Praise for
The Cranberry Cove Mysteries

"Peg Cochran has a truly entertaining writing style that is filled with humor, mystery, fun, and intrigue. You cannot ask for a lot more in a super cozy!"

—Open Book Society

"A fun whodunnit with quirky characters and a satisfying mystery. This new series is as sweet and sharp as the heroine's cranberry salsa."

—Sofie Kelly, *New York Times* bestselling author of the Magical Cats Mysteries

"Cozy fans and foodies rejoice—there's a place just for you and it's called Cranberry Cove."

—Ellery Adams, *New York Times* bestselling author of the Supper Club Mysteries

"I can't wait for Monica's next tasty adventure—and I'm not just saying that because I covet her cranberry relish recipe."

—Victoria Abbott, national bestselling author of the Book Collector Mysteries

Books by Peg Cochran

The Cranberry Cove Mysteries

Berried Secrets
Berry the Hatchet
Dead and Berried
Berried at Sea
Berried in the Past

The Lucille Mysteries

Confession Is Murder
Unholy Matrimony
Hit and Nun
A Room with a Pew
Cannoli to Die For

Farmer's Daughter Mysteries

No Farm, No Foul
Sowed to Death
Bought the Farm

More Books by Peg Cochran

The Gourmet De-Lite Mysteries

Allergic to Death
Steamed to Death
Iced to Death

Murder, She Reported Mysteries

Murder, She Reported
Murder, She Uncovered
Murder, She Encountered

Young Adult Books

Oh, Brother!
Truth or Dare

Writing as Meg London

Murder Unmentionable
Laced with Poison
A Fatal Slip

Berried
in the
Past

A
CRANBERRY COVE
Mystery

Peg Cochran

BEYOND THE PAGE
PUBLISHING

Berried in the Past
Peg Cochran
Beyond the Page Books
are published by
Beyond the Page Publishing
www.beyondthepagepub.com

ISBN: 978-1-950461-41-7

Chapter 1

Monica Albertson slid the curtain aside and looked out the window. It was snowing again, although not as heavily as before. The wind was blowing it into drifts along the side of the road and it was collecting in the corners of the windows. It reminded Monica of when she was a child and she and her mother would spray fake snow on their windows to decorate them at Christmastime.

Individual snowflakes froze to the glass panes, slightly distorting the view outside and turning it hazy, like looking through glass that was wavy with age. The wind whistled fiercely and a frigid draft made its way around the edges of the frame. Monica shivered, let the curtain drop back into place and went to stand by the fire, holding her hands out to warm them.

After a few stalled attempts that had temporarily filled the living room with smoke, they had managed to get a roaring fire going. Flames leapt and danced in the hearth as the fragrant wood crackled and spit.

Monica felt a strong sense of contentment sweep over her and realized she was very lucky indeed. After struggling for a few years running her small café in Chicago, where she sold coffee, tea and her own baked goods, she had agreed to move to Cranberry Cove on the eastern shore of Lake Michigan to help her half brother, Jeff, with his cranberry farm. Jeff had been wounded in Afghanistan and left with a partially paralyzed arm. She did the bookkeeping—having a better head for figures than Jeff—and also ran the farm store, which carried the baked cranberry goods she made. Recently several chain gourmet stores had started carrying Monica's cranberry salsa, putting the farm on slightly more solid footing.

And it was in Cranberry Cove that she'd met her husband, Greg Harper, the owner of Book 'Em, the new and used bookstore in town. She glanced over at Greg, who was ensconced in a comfortable armchair, his feet up on an ottoman, reading the paper. Monica's tuxedo cat, Mittens, was curled up next to him. He must have sensed Monica looking at him because he glanced up and smiled.

Monica had been surprised to find love in such an unlikely place and at an age when she was closer to forty than thirty. It hadn't been a wild, whirlwind romance but rather a slow courtship that had allowed friendship to blossom into love.

They were living in the snug cottage that had been Monica's on Sassamanash Farm. Greg had an apartment over the bookstore, which they eventually planned to turn into the upper floor of Book 'Em with a spiral staircase leading from one floor to the other. Meanwhile, they were studying plans for the house they intended to build on some property Greg owned halfway between the farm and the town.

Monica curled up on the sofa, pulled a knitted throw over her legs and picked up her book.

Lulled by the warmth of the fire and the soothing sound of the crackling of the logs, her eyes began to drift closed. She was nearly asleep when there was a knock on the front door.

Monica's eyes flew open.

Greg looked up from his newspaper. "It's nearly nine o'clock — who would be visiting now . . . and in this weather?"

"I certainly wouldn't be going out in this storm unless absolutely necessary," Monica said, glad to be tucked up warm and cozy at home.

Greg started to get up.

Monica held up a hand. "I'll get it," she said, smiling. "You look so comfortable."

Greg smiled back. "I am, rather."

Monica went out to the small foyer and pulled open the front door.

A gust of wind blew snow across the threshold and the blast of cold air made Monica shiver. She wrapped her arms around herself.

A woman stood on the doorstep. Monica had never seen her before. She was somewhere in her fifties with blond hair cut in a fashionable bob. She was tall and slim and wearing large square black-framed glasses. Her blue eyes behind the lenses looked troubled.

She hadn't buttoned her camel-hair coat but rather was holding it closed with her hand. Monica noticed she was wearing a pair of low-heeled pumps that were totally inappropriate for the weather. It had been snowing for hours, lazily at first and then with greater intensity. Could she have been out and about and caught by surprise? It didn't seem likely.

Monica sensed something *off* about her—not frightening, just peculiar. Her eyes had a vacant look to them and her mouth was moving nervously. She stared at Monica for a moment, opened her mouth and then closed it again. Finally she spoke.

"Someone is trying to kill me."

Chapter 2

A number of thoughts went through Monica's mind as she stood at the open door. Was someone really trying to kill this poor woman? Was she delusional? Was this some sort of ruse to get her to open the door?

The woman was well and expensively dressed. It didn't seem possible that she was part of some sort of gang operation.

Monica felt as if she had hesitated for a very long time but in fact it had merely been several seconds before she invited the woman in.

By now Greg had appeared in the foyer, Mittens at his heels. He raised his eyebrows at Monica but she shook her head.

Together they ushered the woman inside. Greg pulled an armchair closer to the fire and urged her to sit.

The woman collapsed into the chair, hugging her coat around her. Monica could see she was shivering.

"Why don't I make some tea?" she said as the woman continued to sit silently and nearly motionless.

Greg followed Monica to the kitchen, where she filled her ancient teakettle with water, put it on the stove and lit the gas under it.

"I'd put a shot of whiskey in that," Greg said as Monica poured the boiling water over a tea bag in a ceramic mug. "She looks to be in shock." He took another mug from the cupboard. "I think I'll have some of that, too."

"Me, too," Monica said.

Greg reached for another mug. "Did the woman say what her name was? And how she came to knock on our door?"

"No. She said very little actually. But she did say something quite peculiar."

Greg raised his eyebrows.

"She said someone was trying to kill her."

Greg startled and some hot tea sloshed onto his hand. He winced.

"Do you think she's mentally ill?" He ran cold water over his hand.

"I don't know. It does seem awfully far-fetched, doesn't it?" Monica smiled. "Frankly, nothing would surprise me anymore."

They carried the tea out to the living room and Monica handed the woman a mug.

She gave the ghost of a smile as she wrapped her hands around the warm cup. "Thank you."

Her voice was hoarse, as if it was rusty from not speaking for a long time.

"I'm Monica Albertson and this is my husband, Greg," Monica said. She took a sip of her tea and waited.

The woman hesitated for a moment. "I'm Dana Bakker." She looked down. "Thank you for the tea." She glanced at Monica's book laid facedown on the sofa and Greg's newspaper scattered beside his chair. "I'm sorry to have disturbed your evening. I'm afraid my car skidded off the road and is stuck in a snow bank."

Monica noticed Greg's eyes narrow. "We're quite out of the way here on the farm," he said. "Were you lost?"

"Yes." Dana smiled apologetically. "I'm afraid I got turned around in the dark. I—I was in something of a panic." She sighed. "I was hoping I could call a tow truck. I seem to have let my cell phone run down."

Monica tilted her head. "You said someone was trying to kill you," she said as gently as possible. "Do you want to tell us about it? Maybe we can help."

The woman raised a hand and rubbed her forehead. Monica noticed that a plastic hospital bracelet was attached to her wrist.

"I don't remember much. But I do remember someone was trying to kill me." She frowned. "The police thought I had been drinking."

"You've already gone to the police?" Greg said.

Dana shook her head. "No. It was after the accident."

Monica and Greg looked at each other. Greg raised his eyebrows, as if to say *you were right*. The woman must be delusional.

"What accident was that?" Monica said.

"The police said I was speeding—sixty-five miles an hour in a thirty-five-mile-an-hour zone—and driving erratically, weaving in and out of traffic and passing cars on the shoulder." Dana rubbed her forehead again. "I don't remember anything, I'm afraid. They said I hit a tree and they took me to the hospital. Apparently I hit my head on the steering wheel."

"You don't remember the accident at all?" Greg said.

"No. The next thing I remember is waking up in the hospital." She held up her arm with the hospital bracelet on it. "I do know I would never normally drive like that." She gave a small laugh. "I have a perfect driving record, so how could it be?" She shook her head. "No. I do remember I was running from something. I'm certain of it." She looked at them with pleading eyes. "And I'm positive that someone was trying to kill me."

"Do you remember anything at all from before the accident?" Monica set her mug on the coffee table.

"The doctor says I have amnesia—brought on by the blow to my head. All I remember is that I was here—somewhere in Cranberry Cove. The next thing I remember is coming to in the emergency room at the hospital. The rest, I'm afraid, is a blank."

Greg cleared his throat. "You say you remember being here in Cranberry Cove. Do you know when or where?"

Dana took a deep breath. "It had to have been a day or two ago." She glanced at her feet. "I wouldn't go out in a storm in these shoes so it had to have been before the snow started." Dana turned the hospital bracelet around and around on her wrist. "I was at a house. I know that." She smiled apologetically. "I know that isn't much to go on. I think the house had a red front door."

"I don't know that there are too many of those in Cranberry Cove," Greg said.

Monica glanced at him. "Perhaps we can drive around and see if we can locate it." She looked at Dana. "It might jog your memory."

"I don't think we want to go out in this weather." Greg glanced toward the window. "We have a small guest room. Why don't you spend the night? We can go looking tomorrow."

• • •

Monica got Dana settled in their guest room, which barely accommodated a twin bed, nightstand and small dresser, with a stack of fresh towels and one of her own flannel nightgowns. Even with the heat going full blast, the room was chilly, but there was a fluffy down comforter on the bed that ought to keep their guest warm enough throughout the night.

Monica said good night and joined Greg in their bedroom, where he had already changed into his pajamas and was propped up in bed reading.

"Do you think we've done the right thing?" she said as she slipped on her own flannel nightgown. "Letting Dana stay here?"

Greg put his book down. "I think we have. It would have been impossible to get a tow truck out here in a decent amount of time and we could hardly let the poor woman freeze. You don't think she means any harm, do you?"

Monica thought for a moment. "No, I don't. But if someone is really after her and wants to kill her . . . what if they find her here?"

"Frankly, I think she's imagined that part. People can have vivid dreams when they're knocked unconscious. She thinks it's real, but most likely it's not."

Monica slipped under the covers and Mittens jumped up to join her. "You're probably right. I'm worrying for nothing."

She picked up her own book and began to read.

• • •

Monica awoke to the smell of bacon frying. She dressed quickly in a pair of jeans, a warm knitted sweater and socks and ankle boots and went down to the kitchen.

Greg was standing at the stove, an apron tied around his waist, cracking eggs into a frying pan. Once again Monica gave thanks for having a husband as wonderful as Greg.

He turned around and smiled. "Good morning. Breakfast will be ready in a minute."

Monica gave him a kiss and then poured herself a cup of coffee from the pot on the counter. She was stirring in a spoonful of sugar when Dana appeared in the doorway.

Her clothes from the night before were rumpled but she'd obviously run her fingers through her blond hair to get out the tangles and she was wearing a coat of light pink lipstick.

"I'm really being a bother, aren't I?" she said as Monica offered to pour her a cup of coffee.

"Not at all," Greg said, swinging around. "Have a seat—the eggs and bacon are nearly done. Would you like some toast?"

"No, thank you." Dana smiled as she pulled out a chair.

"As soon as we eat, we can head out to see if we can find your house with the red door." Monica glanced toward the window. "The storm is over and the sun's shining. I heard the plows earlier so the roads should be relatively clear."

• • •

Greg had suggested that Monica take his Volvo—it was far from new but it was easier to handle on snow- and ice-covered roads than her Ford Focus, which was even older than his wagon.

Monica bundled up in a bright red parka, gloves and hat. She offered Dana a scarf and also some boots but unfortunately they didn't wear the same size.

The driveway to the cottage had been plowed by one of Jeff's men but Monica still skidded slightly, the rear end of her car fishtailing as she backed out. She remembered her first winter in Cranberry Cove, when she hadn't been nearly as confident driving in the ice and snow. Living in Chicago, she'd depended on public transportation or her own two feet to get around.

Dana was quiet in the passenger seat as they made their way to the main road. Monica hesitated at the crossroads. Which way to go? She decided to head south first, away from Beach Hollow Road and the town center. There were a number of farmhouses in that direction, but for the life of her she couldn't remember whether or not any of them had a front door that had been painted red.

They passed numerous houses with black doors, white doors and even a yellow one, and Monica was about to give up and turn around to head in the other direction when she noticed another house on the horizon. It sat on a slight rise and was surrounded by snow-covered farmland.

She crossed her fingers and headed toward it.

She heard Dana's breath catch in her throat as they approached.

She pointed to the house. "I think that might be it," she said in a shaky voice. They moved closer. "Yes, that's it," Dana said, her voice now excited.

Monica turned down the driveway. It hadn't been plowed recently and there were tire tracks in the snow. She pulled up in front of the house and parked.

Dana had her door open almost before Monica turned off the engine.

She began walking toward the house and mounted the three steps to the front porch that ran the length of the house. The wood was splintered and creaked under her feet.

She stopped with her hand on the doorknob and turned around toward Monica.

"It's coming back to me. At least this part is." She glanced around the porch and took a deep breath. "My sister lives here. The whole family did at one time but we all moved away. Marta was the only one who stayed behind to care for our mother. The poor woman had dementia toward the end."

"Do you think your sister's home?" Monica said, stamping her feet to clear off the snow.

There was no doorbell. Half the door knocker was missing and the remainder was hanging by one screw. Dana raised a hand and rapped sharply against the door. They waited several minutes but no one appeared.

"Perhaps she's gone out?" Monica said.

Dana put her hand on the doorknob. It turned and the door swung inward, creaking on its rusted hinges.

"Marta?" Dana called out.

The small foyer was dark with cabbage rose wallpaper that once must have been bright and cheerful but was now faded and worn. A coatrack made of deer antlers hung on the wall to the left. A lone navy parka with patches on the elbows hung suspended from it. A knitted wool scarf was draped over the jacket.

The living room was small and dominated by a large fireplace. Ashes were piled in the hearth, several scorched logs sat on the andirons, and a poker leaned against the wall.

The sagging sofa was covered with a sheet and the armchair pulled up to the fireplace had a burn mark on the arm.

The most eye-catching piece in the room was an ornate cuckoo clock hanging over the sofa. Monica gestured toward it.

"That's a very unique clock."

"My father made it. He was a woodworker. Frankly, I think it's hideous, but Marta refused to part with it." Dana inclined her head toward the ceiling. "Marta's probably upstairs. She must still be sleeping."

Monica followed Dana up the uneven steps to the second floor, where they headed toward the bedroom at the back of the house.

A double bed with a yellowing candlewick spread bunched at the foot dominated the room. As they approached, they realized a woman was in the bed, lying on her back, her hair spread out around her head.

"It's Marta," Dana whispered. "I hate to wake her, but I have to. I'm sure this is where I was before I lost my memory. I'm hoping she can tell me what happened."

"Marta," Dana called softly as she moved closer to the bed. "It's me, Dana."

There was no response from the figure on the bed.

Dana put her hand on Marta's shoulder and shook her gently.

"Marta," she said again.

Suddenly Dana froze. She bent her head toward Marta, and Monica noticed her place her fingers on her sister's neck.

She whirled around to face Monica, her face drained of color, her eyes wide and horrified.

"I think she's dead."

Chapter 3

"Are you sure?" Monica said, moving toward the bed and Marta's body. She picked up a pillow that had fallen on the floor and replaced it on the bed.

"I don't feel a pulse," Dana said. "Will you check?" She stepped to one side.

Monica put her fingers on Marta's neck and waited. Was that the slight flutter of a heartbeat? She waited, holding her breath, but her fingers failed to detect anything further. She shook her head.

"What do we do?" Dana cried. She clutched the fabric of her coat with both hands.

"We need to call nine-one-one," Monica said, pulling her cell phone from her pocket. "Why don't you sit down while we wait." She motioned toward a straight-backed chair in the corner of the room.

Monica gave the details to the dispatcher and ended the call. She stuck her hands in her pockets. The room was freezing—she wondered if the heating was even turned on.

It wasn't long before they heard a siren in the distance. The wail was cut off abruptly. Monica moved the worn and slightly dingy curtain to the side and looked out. A police car was pulling into the driveway, its tires churning up snow as it made its way toward the house.

"They're here," Monica said.

Dana nodded numbly. She was slumped in the chair, her expression blank, her hands moving restlessly.

"I'm going downstairs to let them in. Will you be okay?"

Dana nodded.

Monica had just reached the foyer when someone pounded on the front door. She opened it and two patrolmen stepped in. Another car came down the drive and pulled in back of the police cruiser. A woman got out.

"Detective Stevens is here," the shorter patrolman said to the other. "Let's wait and see if she needs us."

They stood to the side as Stevens mounted the porch steps. She looked surprised to see Monica. She raised her eyebrows but didn't say anything and silently followed Monica up the steps to the bedroom.

Stevens was wearing a dark puffer coat, and when she took it off at the top of the stairs, Monica was surprised to see how thin she'd become.

Stevens must have noticed Monica's glance. "Chasing a toddler and eating his leftovers because you don't have time to cook is a surprisingly effective diet and exercise plan," she said dryly.

Stevens pulled off her knitted cap, leaving her blond hair slightly ruffled. She smoothed her fingers over it impatiently.

She entered the room and for a few moments was silent as she looked around, then she began to move toward the body on the bed. Much as Dana and Monica had done, Stevens felt for a pulse then shook her head.

"The medical examiner is on the way." She turned toward Monica. "Who is this?" She motioned toward Marta's body.

Dana stepped forward out of the shadows. "It's my sister, Marta Kuiper."

Stevens pulled a notebook and pen from her pocket. They waited while she scribbled down the name.

"And you are?" She looked at Dana.

"Dana Bakker. I live in East Lansing. I'm the registrar at the university there."

Stevens raised her eyebrows. "Address?"

Dana wet her lips. She gave Stevens her address.

"She was dead when you got here?"

Dana shook her head but didn't say anything.

"Yes, she was," Monica said quickly.

Stevens looked at Dana. "She's your sister. So I assume you just happened to stop by for a visit?" she said.

Dana's eyes darted back and forth between Monica and Stevens. "Yes," she said finally. "And we found poor Marta like that."

"Had she been ill?" Stevens said, more gently now.

"I don't know. I don't think so. It might have been her heart. She did say the doctor found something wrong with it but she said he prescribed medication and she was feeling better."

"Do you know who her doctor is?"

"No, I'm afraid not. We used to go to Dr. Krause when we were children, but he would be in his nineties by now if he's even still alive."

Stevens paced around the room. She picked up a pill caddy that was on the nightstand by the bed, then put it down again. She opened the drawer in the nightstand and took out a prescription pill bottle.

She frowned. "These were prescribed by a Dr. Thomas." She pulled her cell phone from her pocket and dialed the number on the bottle. "Chances are he's your sister's doctor."

Five minutes later she ended the call and returned her phone to her pocket.

"It seems that Dr. Thomas has been treating your sister for high blood pressure and pulmonary hypertension. He believes it's likely she died of natural causes, but we still have to see what the ME says."

Moments later they heard footsteps on the stairs and a man burst into the room. He was wearing a cashmere tweed coat with a velvet collar and had a silk scarf carefully tied at his neck.

"Where's the body?" he said brusquely, glancing around the room. He glanced at his watch, a slim gold affair. "I have to catch a flight within the hour. I'm attending a conference in Arizona and I can't wait to get away from this blasted cold and snow."

Stevens motioned toward the bed and the ME hurried in that direction.

"Was she under a doctor's care?" He looked over his shoulder at Stevens.

"Yes."

He looked annoyed. "Then you probably don't need me." He pulled on a pair of rubber gloves and began to examine the body. "No evident signs of trauma. This room is freezing so rigor mortis would have been delayed, but it's already passed, so I'd say the poor thing has been lying here for anywhere from two to four days."

He snapped off his gloves and handed them to Stevens.

"No need for an autopsy. Death from natural causes." He picked up his bag and stomped from the room.

Stevens waited until she heard his footsteps on the stairs. She turned to Dana.

"That's it, I guess. You can call the funeral parlor now."

Dana nodded. "I'm going to call my brother first. There may be arrangements already in place . . . I don't know."

Stevens nodded. She touched Monica's arm. "Good to see you again."

• • •

Dana had started to shiver.

"Why don't we go downstairs," Monica said. "I can see about making us a hot cup of tea."

Dana didn't argue and followed Monica down the stairs to the living room, where she perched on the end of the sofa as if she was going to jump up and run away at any minute.

The kitchen was as bleak as the rest of the house — the appliances were avocado green, which led Monica to suspect they hadn't been replaced since at least the nineteen-seventies. The Formica counter was scarred and stained with a raised burn mark in the shape of a circle near the stove. It looked as if someone had set a hot pan directly on it.

Monica rummaged in the cupboards until she found two mismatched mugs, a handful of tea bags and a bowl of sugar with a crust on top. There was no microwave. She located a pan, boiled some water and poured it over the tea bags. As the water darkened to a deep mahogany color, she added generous amounts of sugar and carried the mugs out to the living room.

"I'm so sorry. This must be terribly hard for you," she said to Dana as she handed her the tea. Dana cradled the mug and held her face to the steam rising from the hot liquid. She had stopped shivering.

"Marta and I were once very close, although not as much recently. We ended up leading different lives — we lived in different worlds. She was my older sister, my only sister, and she always looked after me when we were growing up. Our mother often wasn't well — she got terrible migraines — and Marta would make dinner for John and me. Nothing fancy — hot dogs and beans, spaghetti with sauce from a can, things like that. But she always made sure we had something to eat."

Dana took a sip of her tea. She stared into the distance for several seconds. "I did well in school and I wanted to go to college. All my teachers encouraged me. Our mother had early-onset dementia and Marta stepped in to take care of her so John and I could continue our studies. John became a heart surgeon. I was even married briefly. That wouldn't have been possible if it hadn't been for Marta."

A tear rolled down Dana's cheek.

"John is my older brother. We're only sixteen months apart—Irish twins, they used to call us. Two pregnancies so close together put quite a strain on our mother. I always wondered if it didn't contribute to her migraines."

She pulled a tissue from her purse and dabbed at her eyes. "I suppose I should call John."

She retrieved her phone from her pocket and punched in some numbers.

"He's leaving right now," she said when she ended the call. "He's about an hour away. He works at the Fred and Lena Meijer Heart Center in Grand Rapids."

While they waited, Monica checked the thermostat and found she was right, the heating had been turned off. How peculiar. Perhaps Marta turned it off when she went to bed at night? She knew she and Greg lowered the temperature before going to sleep.

Monica set the thermostat to seventy degrees and went out to the kitchen to clean up the tea things.

Dana was sitting on the couch in the same position when Monica returned to the living room. She took a seat in the armchair and leaned toward Dana, her elbows resting on her knees.

"Why didn't you tell Detective Stevens that you thought someone was trying to kill you?" Monica said softly.

Dana jerked as if waking from a dream.

"Why? Because I knew she wouldn't believe me. She would think I was crazy just like the doctors at the hospital did." She glanced down at her hands. "They sent a psychiatrist to examine me. And I heard them talking about transferring me to a psychiatric hospital. I . . . I couldn't let them do that." She gave a bitter smile. "I guess you could say I escaped. As soon as I was alone I changed into my clothes and walked out."

• • •

Not quite an hour later they heard a car outside and tires churning up the icy driveway.

"That must be John," Dana said, getting up.

Monica went to the window and saw a late-model bottle green Jaguar negotiating the long snowy drive. Its driver was clearly impatient, stepping on the gas as the car became stuck in a rut and sending its tires spinning furiously. Finally the car jolted forward and the driver pulled up to the house and parked.

Soon they heard footsteps on the front porch, boots stomping and a loud rap against the front door. John didn't wait for an answer but pushed the door open and stepped into the foyer.

He was in his fifties, tall and trim with thick silver hair swept back from a high forehead and an imperious expression. A woman entered the room behind him. She was clearly at least twenty years younger and was wearing an improbable outfit given the slush and snow outside—a dark brown leather coat and thigh-high suede boots. Her hair was long and blond and two words immediately came to mind when Monica saw her—*expensive* and *high-maintenance.*

"What's this all about?" John said as he stood at the entrance to the room.

Dana took a step toward him, one hand outstretched. "It's Marta, I'm afraid. She's dead." Dana sniffed and pulled a tissue from her pocket.

"You called Dr. Thomas, I presume?" John pulled off his leather gloves and stuffed them in his pockets.

"Yes. He seems to think it was her heart."

"And you disagree with his diagnosis?"

Dana took a step backward. "I—I . . ."

What a bully, Monica thought.

John's expression softened slightly. "I suppose it was to be expected given the condition of her heart. Was she taking her medication regularly?"

"There was a pill caddy on her nightstand," Monica said. "It appeared to be well organized."

He glanced at Monica. "Who are you?" John raised his

eyebrows. "And what are you doing here?" He looked at Dana with a stony expression.

"This is Monica Albertson," Dana said. "She's a . . . friend." Dana looked at Monica, her eyes pleading.

Monica had no intention of betraying Dana's secret. She didn't know why, but she didn't trust John—it was a gut feeling. It wasn't his arrogance that had brought her to that conclusion, but something else she couldn't quite put her finger on.

The woman with John still hadn't said a word. Monica noticed a large diamond solitaire along with a diamond band on the ring finger of her left hand, so Monica assumed she was John's wife. He obviously couldn't be bothered to introduce her.

Dana seemed to sense Monica's thoughts. "Monica, this is my sister-in-law, Tiffany," she said.

Tiffany was certainly aptly named, Monica thought. Besides the bling on her ring finger, she was wearing diamond studs and a heavy gold bracelet that clinked when she moved her arm.

"Have you called the funeral parlor?" John said. "They need to be notified to come and get the body."

He breathed out heavily through his nose, reminding Monica of a thoroughbred at the gate impatient to get on with the race.

Dana looked as if someone had thrown cold water at her. "Not yet. I don't know if Marta made any prior arrangements. Perhaps there's something among her papers."

"I don't think we need to waste time on that," John snapped. "There must be an outfit in town we can call."

Monica cleared her throat. "There's Mingledorff and Hoogerwerf. They've been in Cranberry Cove for more than a hundred years."

"I imagine they'll do." John snapped his fingers at Dana. "Best get them on the phone."

Dana's hand shook as she held her phone.

"Let me do it," Monica said. She retrieved her own phone, did a search for the telephone number and punched it in.

The woman on the other end at Mingledorff and Hoogerwerf was professionally sympathetic but also efficient. She took down all the information and promised to send someone to retrieve the body of the deceased immediately.

"Everything seems to be in order," John said when Monica ended the call. "I'll be leaving. I've some medical journals to catch up on and then I have a surgery scheduled for later this afternoon."

Monica waited while Dana walked John and Tiffany to the door and said goodbye.

"I'm sorry about my brother," Dana said as soon as she joined Monica in the living room again. "He doesn't mean to be rude. It's the pressures of his job. I can't imagine holding someone else's life in my hands and that's what he does every single day."

Monica felt like uttering a few choice words but she restrained herself. Dana wasn't responsible for John's behavior.

She waved a hand. "It's fine. Please don't worry about it."

But Monica wasn't entirely convinced that John had been simply rude. She had the feeling that he'd been scared.

But scared of what?

Chapter 4

Delicious smells were coming from the kitchen when Monica opened the back door to her cottage. She slipped off her boots and went to stand next to Greg, who was hovering over something on the stove.

"That smells heavenly," Monica said, realizing for the first time that she was hungry. "What is it?"

Greg smiled and kissed Monica on the cheek. "Smokey chipotle chili," he said, giving the pot a stir. "I thought we'd have it with some of your cranberry corn bread."

"You spoil me," Monica said, giving him a quick hug.

She hung up her coat, put her hat and gloves on the shelf and went to the cupboard for place mats and napkins.

"I hope that will be ready soon. I'm starving."

"It's ready just as soon as you are," Greg said, lowering the flame under the pot.

Greg filled bowls with chili while Monica warmed the cranberry corn bread in the oven. She carried it to the table along with a tub of fresh butter.

"Did you find the mysterious house with the red door?" Greg said as he unfurled his napkin and placed it on his lap.

"We did. It turned out to be Dana's childhood home. Her sister lives . . . lived there."

"Lived?" Greg's eyebrows rose. "Don't tell me—"

"Yes. Sadly, we found she'd passed away. The doctor was treating her for a heart condition."

"Natural causes then? No foul play? No blunt instrument?"

Monica could tell Greg was teasing—she'd been involved in more than her share of murders. Tempest Storm, who ran the new age shop in town, said there had to be something in her aura that attracted death. Monica hoped she was wrong—not that she really believed in things like that. She was far too pragmatic and practical.

"Not even an autopsy," Monica said. "The ME believed it to be natural causes. Although he was in such a hurry, I wonder how he could be sure."

"How is Dana coping? Did her memory come back?"

"She seems to be doing okay. Her brother didn't help—what an obnoxious so-and-so." Monica picked up her spoon. "She did remember the house when she saw it. And she recognized it and her sister. But the accident is still a blur to her. She doesn't remember a thing."

"Will she be coming back to stay here?" Greg dug into his chili.

Monica jerked around to look at him. "But Greg, we—"

He held up a hand. "I know. But you said you would think about it."

"No. She'll be staying at her sister's house until the funeral is over."

"So. Life goes back to normal then."

"Yes," Monica said, but she had the feeling that this was far from over.

$$\bullet \ \bullet \ \bullet$$

Monica was stripping the sheets off the bed in the guest room—she'd toss them in the washer in the morning while she waited for the coffee to brew—when Greg came up behind her.

He put his arms around her waist. "You know," he said softly, "this would make a good room for a baby. At least until we build our house."

Monica bit her lip. It wasn't that she didn't *want* a baby or was opposed to the idea of having one. It had just never occurred to her. After all, she'd never expected to marry—she'd been engaged once but her fiancé had been killed in an accident, and after that she'd had her share of dates but nothing had ever come of them. The idea of a *baby* had never even crossed her mind.

Monica looked around the room trying to picture a crib against the far wall, a small dresser painted pink or blue and maybe a rocking chair in the corner.

She frowned. "Greg, I don't want us to get our hopes up. I'm afraid I might be too old . . ."

"We won't know until we try, will we?"

Monica looked up at Greg's face. "You won't be disappointed in me if it doesn't work out?"

Greg smiled, put his finger under Monica's chin and tilted her face up.

"I could never be disappointed in you."

• • •

Monica normally jumped out of bed the minute the alarm went off if not before. Mittens could be counted on to make sure she didn't oversleep—frequently Monica's wake-up call was the cat sitting on her chest and patting her face with a paw.

Today, however, the room was chilly and the bed was deliciously warm. Monica pulled the comforter up further and burrowed beneath it.

But she didn't stay long. She had a busy day—and a busy week—ahead of her. And when duty called, Monica generally answered.

In order to provide fresh stock for the Sassamanash farm store, she had to be up early to start baking. A small group of customers, on their way to work, often stopped in for a warm muffin or scone and mothers would be in a bit later, after dropping their children off at school, for baked goods for their families.

She dressed quickly in warm clothes—the weatherman was predicting temperatures in the low teens—and headed down to the kitchen with Mittens at her heels.

She filled the coffee maker and turned it on, yawning as the water began to trickle into the pot. She heard Greg's feet hit the floor overhead and then the sound of the shower running.

She put the sheets from the guest room in the washer and went to turn it on, but paused with her hand on the knob, remembering her conversation with Greg the night before. She shook her head. This wasn't the time to think about it. She had to get to work.

Mittens appeared and meowed loudly. Monica went back to the kitchen, put food in the bowl for Mittens and began scrambling some eggs.

Greg came downstairs as Monica was finishing the last bit of her breakfast.

"I've got to go," she said, pushing back her chair and carrying her dishes to the sink. She rinsed them and put them in the dishwasher. "There are still some cranberry scones if you'd like.

And I left some scrambled eggs in the pan. You just have to warm them up a bit." Monica gestured toward the stove. "And would you mind throwing those sheets in the dryer when the washer stops?"

"Sure, no problem. And thanks." Greg kissed her on the cheek. "You take such good care of me."

Monica put on all her winter gear — parka, hat, scarf, gloves and boots — and with a final goodbye to Greg headed out the door.

The cold nearly took her breath away but it swept away any last remaining vestiges of sleepiness. She buried her hands in her pockets and hunched her shoulders as she walked from her cottage to the commercial kitchen Jeff had built on the farm when Monica's cranberry products began to take off.

The snow crunched under her feet as she headed down the path past the cranberry bogs — dark smudges against the sky, which was beginning to lighten ever so slightly. The delicate vines were protected from the cold by a thick layer of ice and soon Jeff and his men would be spreading sand on top. As the ice melted, the sand would sift into the trenches, choking out the opportunistic weeds that would appear in the spring.

The interior of the farm kitchen, which smelled of sugar, baked dough and cranberries, was still chilled from the frigid temperatures of the night before, but it began to warm up nicely as soon as Monica cranked up the heat.

She hung up her jacket and took her chef's apron from a hook by the counter. She planned to start with some muffins and scones, which were the products most in demand by their early morning customers. Later on she would start work on the chocolate chip cranberry walnut cookies that had become a favorite.

Empty wooden crates stamped with *Sassamanash Farm* were stacked against the wall. The cranberries had been transferred to the freezer for the long winter until the next crop was harvested.

A blast of cold air swept across the room. Monica looked up. Her assistant, Kit Tanner, had just arrived. His cheeks were red from the cold and he was blowing on his hands to warm them.

"A bit nippy out today," Monica said.

"Yeah." Kit hung up his jacket.

Monica was surprised. Kit's greeting was usually more effusive and accompanied by a broad smile. There was no smile today.

Kit had started working for Monica in the fall and had proven himself to be an enormous help. He was a talented baker — efficient, organized and trustworthy — with a flair for creating new recipes.

At first, Jeff had been put off by Kit's appearance — he was slim and wore his black hair shaved up the sides and long enough on top to flop onto his forehead — but Monica had been taken with Kit and had persuaded Jeff to give him a chance. Neither had been sorry.

"Is everything okay?" Monica said as Kit measured flour into the mixer. The bracelets on his wrist jingled as he worked.

"Yes, darling, I'm fine. Do stop worrying," Kit said, standing with one hand on his cocked hip.

Monica wasn't convinced. Something was clearly wrong. Kit was definitely not his usual self. She decided to drop the subject for the moment and got started on a batch of scones. She mixed the dough, spread flour on the counter and then began to roll it out.

She was putting the scones in the oven when Kit suddenly said, "Okay, if you must know, Sean and I had a wee little spat last night and I'm still upset."

"I'm sorry," Monica said, trying to conceal her surprise at Kit's sudden confession. "I hope it wasn't serious."

Kit pursed his lips and made a face. "All I can say is he needs to apologize . . . stat." He pushed his lower lip out further.

"I hope the two of you make up."

"I hope so, too," Kit said, but his tone was glum. "Say" — his face brightened — "I heard you found another body. Girl, I'm beginning to think you're bad luck." He grinned to show he was kidding.

"Yes, but it's not what you think. This time it was natural causes," Monica said.

Kit must have picked up on the note of doubt in her voice.

"You don't sound convinced." He turned toward Monica with his hands on his hips. He had a bit of flour on the end of his nose and she had to resist the urge to laugh.

"You have to ask yourself who benefits. Did the deceased have any money?"

"I don't think so," Monica said. "She owned a farmhouse and a good amount of land down off Bluff Road."

Kit whistled. "Darling, property *is* money. Is there a view?"

"You do get a glimpse of the lake up that high. I suppose someone might buy it. But the house can't be worth very much— it's not in the best repair."

"Are you kidding? Developers are gobbling up places like that and building shopping malls and gigantic new developments with hideously tacky houses. Cranberry Cove is ripe for the picking for something like that, if you'll pardon the pun." He giggled.

"I hadn't thought of that."

That certainly put a new spin on things, Monica thought. Had someone approached Marta about selling her property? And if so, who would stand to benefit now that she was dead?

• • •

Monica forgot about Dana and Marta as she worked through the morning, pulling sheet after sheet of cranberry scones from the oven and glazing the tops with drizzles of icing.

She whipped up some batter for muffins, added cranberries and filled the muffin tins. Once they were out of the oven, she glazed them with a confectioner's sugar icing and sprinkled chopped candied walnuts on top. It was a new recipe she'd decided to try, and so far their customers had responded enthusiastically.

Once Monica had everything ready, she filled trays with the baked goods and put them on a cart. She pulled on her jacket, hat and gloves.

"I'm taking these down to the store," she yelled to Kit.

The kitchen had become quite warm with the ovens going full tilt for several hours. The blast of cold air when Monica opened the door sent a shiver down her spine and she was glad she didn't have a long walk.

The farm store was on the other side of the cranberry processing building, a wooden shingled structure with a small parking lot out front for customers.

The short walk had been enough to get her blood flowing, and she peeled off her parka as soon as she reached the store and got inside. Monica had recently added three small tables and chairs where customers could sit and drink a cup of coffee and enjoy a muffin or other breakfast treat. All the tables were full and several more people were on line at the counter.

Nora, the woman who helped in the shop, smiled when she saw Monica.

"Reinforcements! Wonderful. We're nearly out of muffins and scones from the freezer."

"Are these freshly baked?" a woman in a camel-hair coat asked.

"They're still warm," Monica said as she shifted the trays from the cart to the glass bakery case.

Nora filled the woman's order and placed two muffins and two scones in a white paper bag.

"Those muffins look delicious," Nora said to Monica as she rang up the sale.

"It's something new I'm trying," Monica said, slicing a loaf of cranberry bread and arranging the slices on a silver tray she'd picked up at an estate sale. "Fingers crossed they go over well."

"I'm sure they will," Nora said, eyeing the muffins in the case. "I'm dying to have one, but sadly they aren't included in my diet." She patted her stomach and smiled.

There was a momentary lull after the customers left and then the door opened again.

Monica looked up from the receipts she was going through.

"Oh," she said.

It was Dana. She'd changed her clothes, Monica noticed. She was wearing a sweater Monica had seen in the window of Danielle's on Beach Hollow Road, a chunky knit pullover in a vivid royal blue. Monica had gone into the shop to check the price even though she knew beforehand it would not be in her budget.

Dana smiled nervously as she approached the counter. "I was wondering if you had a minute? There's something I'd like you to see," she said to Monica. "It's at my sister's house if that's not too much trouble. The tow truck finally got my car unstuck so I can drive you if you'd like."

Monica looked at Nora.

"Go on." Nora flapped a hand at Monica. "I can handle things."

"Okay, sure. I'll get my coat," Monica said.

She followed Dana to the parking lot, where Dana pulled out

her keys and beeped open a late-model BMW parked at the end of a row.

Monica slid into the front passenger seat. The car was luxurious inside and smelled of leather. Monica ran her hands over the seat — she knew she'd never have a car like this but that was okay with her.

The sun was up now and ice was beginning to melt off the tree branches with a steady drip-drip, although the piles of snow pushed to the side of the road by the plows probably wouldn't be gone until the spring.

The heat was on in the farmhouse, making it feel slightly more hospitable but no less grim. The bright sun coming through the window only illuminated the bare patches on the sofa and the frayed spots on the rug.

"Would you like some tea?" Dana said. She unwound her scarf and tossed it and her coat on a chair.

"That would be lovely," Monica said, following Dana to the kitchen.

Dana swung the teakettle under the tap, filled it with water and put it on the stove. She turned the gas on underneath.

"Our father died before our mother did. Even though she had dementia, she managed to outlive him. I think his death pushed her even further into the world she'd escaped into."

Dana took two tea bags and two mugs from the cupboard.

"My father was very old-fashioned. He and my mother took care of each other. I don't see why people nowadays look askance at that. He worked and handled the finances, she took care of the children and cooked and cleaned."

She paused as she retrieved the kettle and poured water over the tea bags.

"On the other hand, it did make my mother very dependent on him for certain things. She had no idea how to balance a checkbook or even how to write a check. But by then it hardly mattered since she was no longer capable of those things even if she had known how to do them."

Dana carried the mugs to the kitchen table and sat down. A stack of papers was next to her elbow.

"The house was left to us three children but with the provision that Marta would be allowed to live in it until she died." Dana shuddered. "Frankly, I couldn't wait to get away from here, but Marta never minded. She'd become isolated—taking care of our mother—and seemed uncomfortable whenever she had to leave to go somewhere."

Dana took a sip of her tea.

"Which brings me to these papers." She pulled the stack by her elbow in front of her. "I found this among Marta's things." She handed a letter to Monica.

Monica scanned it swiftly and then handed it back.

"So a developer wanted to buy the property from Marta?"

"It appears so," Dana said. She pushed another set of papers toward Monica.

Monica looked through them and nearly gasped when she saw the sum the developer was offering.

"The developer, Shoreline Development, apparently wants to build a mall here."

Monica couldn't imagine it. There would be more traffic, and the small shops on Beach Hollow Road would suffer. It would change Cranberry Cove, and not necessarily for the better.

"Was Marta planning to sell?" Monica said, handing the paper back to Dana.

"I don't know."

"I do." John walked into the room and they both jumped.

"I didn't hear you come in," Dana said, gathering the papers together quickly.

John pulled off his leather gloves and slapped them down on the table. He pulled out a chair and sat down, loosening his coat.

"I came to see about the funeral arrangements," he said. "I had a consultation nearby and didn't want to waste my time coming back."

"So you knew about the developer wanting to buy Marta's house?" Dana said, looking at John. "You never said."

"Our house," John said. "Marta had life rights, but the house and property belonged to the three of us."

"So we would all have had to agree to sell?" Dana said.

"Yes," John said. He picked up his gloves and began playing with them. "But Marta refused to sell so there was no point in discussing it any further. That's why I never mentioned it." He ran a hand through his hair, sweeping it back from his high forehead. "I tried to convince her that selling would be for her own good. There's a retirement place near me where she could have bought a modern apartment, had her meals in the dining room and been surrounded by people instead of stuck here all alone. But she refused to even consider it." He stood up and pulled on his gloves. "But now with Marta gone, there's nothing to stop us from accepting the developer's deal."

Afterward, Monica couldn't help but wonder whether Dana really hadn't known about the offer for the house and farm earlier. And whether John had really taken Marta's refusal to sell so readily.

Chapter 5

Dana was turning out the lights and Monica was about to put on her coat when there was a tentative knock on the front door. Dana went to answer it.

An older woman was standing on the doorstep. "Dana," she said. "What a pleasant surprise."

Dana held the door wider and the woman stepped into the living room.

"Monica, this is Joyce Murphy, an old friend of Marta's. You knew each other when you were teenagers, didn't you?" Dana said.

"Yes. Marta and I go way back. We met in elementary school and have been friends ever since."

"I'm afraid I have some bad news," Dana said. She motioned toward the sofa. "Why don't you sit down."

"What is it, dear?" Joyce said, her voice trembling slightly. She fingered the homemade-looking bead necklace around her neck. She must have noticed Monica looking at it. "My granddaughter made this for me."

"I'm afraid Marta has passed away," Dana said as gently as possible.

Joyce gasped and put a hand to her chest. "Oh, no. Poor dear Marta." She pulled a tissue from the sleeve of her sweatshirt and blew her nose. "Was it her heart?"

"We think so," Dana said.

"It's hard to believe. She seemed fine when I saw her. We had tea together. I tried to look in on her every day seeing as how we're both alone." She fingered her necklace again. "I was just leaving when your brother John arrived. He seemed upset about something." Joyce began to shred the tissue in her hand. "I had barely closed the front door when I heard them start arguing."

She put a hand to her face. It was trembling. "I almost went back inside. He was being positively awful to her. I felt terrible for her."

• • •

Monica shuddered at the thought of getting out of Dana's luxuriously warm car — even the seats were heated — as they neared Sassamanash Farm. The skies were still blue and sunny but the wind had increased and was shimmying the car slightly as they drove along Bluff Road.

Finally, Dana pulled onto the winding drive to the farm and up to the farm store and Monica had no choice but to get out of the car. She pulled her jacket more closely around her as she opened the door. The wind grabbed the door and nearly yanked it from her hand.

She thanked Dana and dashed for the shelter of the store.

The shop was empty except for one customer, a woman in yoga pants sitting at one of the café tables nursing a cup of coffee.

Nora was swabbing down one of the tables and turned around when she heard the door open.

"It doesn't look as if you need any help," Monica said. "I thought I'd bake up another few batches of cookies for this afternoon and I've got to get to work on the cranberry compote the Pepper Pot ordered." Monica felt a slight thrill at the thought. "They've created a new dessert that uses our compote, cinnamon ice cream and dark chocolate shavings. They're calling it Sassamanash Farm Delight."

"That's wonderful." Nora smiled, highlighting the fine lines around her eyes. "Go on, then. I'll be fine. I suspect we'll need the cookies for the afternoon crowd anyway."

Monica took a deep breath, opened the door and stepped back outside. The wind tore at her scarf and blew it across her face. She nearly slipped on a patch of ice as she pulled it away from her eyes. She was definitely going to be glad when spring arrived.

Someone was coming toward her in the distance. As the figure got closer, Monica realized it was Jeff. He was struggling to hold a stack of boxes under his right arm — his injured left arm hanging nearly useless at his side.

Suddenly the boxes began to slip and eventually all of them tumbled to the ground.

Monica could hear him swear as he bent and tried to pick them up. She waved and hurried forward.

Jeff looked up. "Hey, Sis."

Jeff had always called Monica *Sis*, and even though they'd only spent part of their time together when Monica visited her father and stepmother, Gina, they'd always been close.

"Let me help," Monica said.

Jeff stood up and scowled. "It stinks," he said, kicking at one of the boxes and sending it spinning.

"I imagine it must be frustrating," Monica said soothingly.

Jeff's face was red and his right hand was clenched at his side.

"I can't do anything with my arm like this. It's not fair." He kicked at another one of the boxes.

Monica hadn't seen Jeff act like this for a long while now. When he'd first returned from Afghanistan, he'd been quite bitter and Monica had been worried about him. But over time—and with the help of his fiancée, Lauren—the bitterness had faded and been replaced by acceptance. As the farm took off and became more prosperous, Monica would have almost said that Jeff seemed happy, especially when he and Lauren became engaged.

But now some of his anger at his injury seemed to have returned.

Together they gathered up the remaining boxes.

"Where to?" Monica said.

"The processing shed if you don't mind walking over there." Jeff gave a slight smile. "I can see you're cold." He laughed. "Your cheeks are all red."

Monica's hand flew to her face. "I'm fine," she said as she fell into step beside him.

"You look good," Jeff said. "You look happy."

Monica took a deep breath. "I am. Greg is . . . wonderful. I'm still surprised at how lucky I've been."

"You deserve it." Jeff sighed. "I can only hope Lauren and I will be as happy as you and Greg are."

"You're well-suited to each other. I think you will be."

The processing plant was quiet. The fall crop had long since been harvested, processed, packaged and shipped. Jeff spent the winter months tending to the equipment, doing maintenance work and repairs, to be ready for the next growing season.

"Can I talk to you, Sis?" Jeff said after they'd stacked the boxes on a worktable.

"Sure. Shoot." Monica pulled off her gloves and loosened her scarf.

"I read about this new therapy that's supposed to treat injuries like mine." Jeff indicated his left arm. "I don't pretend to understand it, but it has something to do with stem cells."

"It's experimental?" Monica raised an eyebrow.

Jeff hesitated. "Yes. But it seems there isn't much risk with the procedure. The real downside is that it doesn't always work."

"So you're thinking about it?" Monica said, her brow creased.

Jeff's expression wasn't readable. "Maybe," he said. He scowled and kicked at a box on the floor. "This morning I had to ask Lauren to help me button my shirt. Normally I can manage by myself, but today my fingers wouldn't cooperate." He ducked his head. "I felt like a fool."

"I'm sure Lauren didn't mind."

"That's the thing." Jeff looked Monica in the eye. "I'm afraid she'll get tired of having to help me all the time, that she'll go off and find somebody who has two functioning arms."

Jeff squared his shoulders. "If I can get that therapy, I'm going to do it. I don't care what it takes."

• • •

Monica had just gotten back to her cottage when her cell phone rang. She put the groceries she'd purchased on the table and reached into her pocket.

The call was from Dana. She wanted to thank Monica and Greg for their hospitality and for all they'd done for her and invited them to dinner at the Pepper Pot.

Monica thought of the chicken she'd picked up at Bart's Butcher but decided it could easily go in the refrigerator for another night and accepted the invitation. She didn't think Greg would mind.

Moments later the back door opened and Greg walked in, stomping his boots to rid them of the last bits of snow clinging to them.

"We've been invited out to dinner," Monica said, kissing his cheek, which was cold to the touch. "Dana wants to take us out as a way of saying thank you."

Greg smiled. "I'm not going to argue with that. When?"

"I said we'd meet her at the Pepper Pot in an hour. She's made a reservation."

"Time enough then for a glass of wine." Greg hung his coat on the hook by the door. "Shall I pour you one?"

"Sounds heavenly. Meanwhile, I'm going to spruce up a bit."

Monica looked down at herself—her sweater was smudged with flour and she hadn't even thought about combing her hair or touching up her lipstick all day.

She'd never been one to linger in front of the mirror, fussing with makeup or trying different hairstyles. A quick bit of powder on her nose, a slick of lipstick and a comb pulled through her hair usually sufficed in her opinion.

She changed from her jeans and sweater into a pair of black pants and her good cashmere sweater. Greg had a glass of wine waiting for her when she got downstairs.

"Drink up," he said, reaching down to scratch Mittens, who was rubbing up against his leg looking for some attention. "We'd best be leaving soon."

• • •

The night sky was clear and sprinkled with stars. Monica huddled in her coat, her hand warm in Greg's, as they scurried from the parking lot to the Pepper Pot. A blast of heat hit them when they opened the door to the restaurant and they were bathed in mouthwatering smells.

The Pepper Pot specialized in comfort food with a slight gourmet twist and had been a welcome addition to the Cranberry Cove culinary scene, which previously had consisted solely of the Cranberry Cove Diner and the Cranberry Cove Inn.

The hostess smiled at them and motioned for them to follow her, letting them know that their party had already arrived.

Dana was seated at a table with a glass of wine at her elbow. She was perusing the menu and looked up when they approached. She removed the reading glasses perched on the end of her nose and stood up to shake their hands.

She was smartly dressed in a black and white tweed sheath

with a matching jacket. The confused look in her eyes was gone and she looked alert and focused.

The waiter appeared immediately and handed around menus. Monica's stomach grumbled as she looked at hers. It was a treat to have someone else prepare dinner for a change. Everything looked so good she wasn't sure how she would decide.

Greg snapped his menu shut.

"You've decided?" Monica said.

"I'm having the steak frites," he said. "Rib eye medium rare with French fries."

Monica was still wavering but finally settled on the chicken with roasted winter vegetables.

They made pleasant conversation until the waiter arrived with their drinks, wine for Monica and a whiskey and soda for Greg. As soon as the waiter left the table, Dana reached for her purse and pulled out a piece of paper.

She looked apologetic. "I know this was meant to be a convivial evening, but I wanted to show this to you." She put a piece of paper on the table and smoothed it out. "This is a receipt from the Cranberry Cove drugstore for one of Marta's prescriptions. I found it rather odd. It's for a beta blocker. That's a pill that's taken for high blood pressure or other heart irregularities."

She turned the paper around so Monica and Greg could see it.

"The odd thing is I couldn't find any of these pills in Marta's bedroom, or anywhere else in the house, for that matter."

Monica frowned. "That is odd. But do you think there's anything questionable about it? People lose things all the time. So why not a bottle of pills? Maybe she forgot them at the drugstore or left them somewhere?"

"We talked to one of Marta's friends," Dana said, putting the receipt back in her purse. "Remember, Monica? Joyce saw Marta earlier in the day and said she seemed fine. She was out shoveling snow, for heaven's sake."

"Are you thinking there was something fishy about Marta's death?" Greg said, tossing back the last of his whiskey.

"Joyce did say she heard Marta and your brother arguing." Monica helped herself to one of the olives the waiter had brought with their drinks.

Dana ran her finger around the rim of her wineglass. "I don't know. It's only a feeling."

She sat up a bit straighter. "Yes. I think there is something fishy about it." She rubbed her forehead. "If only I could remember what happened right before I had that accident. I'm sure it's connected to Marta's death somehow."

Chapter 6

Monica wiped the sleep from her eyes and pulled on a pair of vinyl gloves. She reached for a bowl of dough that she'd covered with a clean dish towel. The dough had doubled in size, and when she removed the cloth the scent of yeast filled the air.

She was reaching for the flour to spread on the counter when her cell phone rang. She was about to let it go to voice mail when she realized the call might be from Greg. She yanked off her gloves, took her cell phone from her pocket and answered slightly breathlessly.

"Monica? This is Dana." A slight pause and then, "I hope I'm not bothering you."

"No," Monica said, glancing at the clock.

"You know how I found that receipt for a prescription of beta blockers for Marta?"

"Yes. Did you find the bottle of pills?"

"No. And as a matter of fact, I went through Marta's pill caddy, which was still half full, and there were no beta blockers in it. I had the devil of a time identifying all the pills from some pictures online, but I'm quite certain none of them was the beta blocker."

"Perhaps it was a new prescription?" The thought had just occurred to Monica.

"No. According to the receipt, it was a refill. I've done some research . . ."

Monica could hear papers rustling.

"According to an online medical source, an overdose of beta blockers can cause a slowing of the heartbeat and difficulty breathing. If not treated, it can be fatal."

The word *fatal* hung in the air for several seconds.

"You think Marta was murdered?" Monica said.

"I don't know what to think. I told you I thought something was fishy about it."

"Could Marta have taken an overdose by accident?"

"I don't see how. All her pills are arranged in the pill caddy. Plus, the beta blockers are nowhere to be found." There was a lengthy silence. "Do you think I should go to the police?"

The question took Monica by surprise. So far all this had been mere speculation. She had to admit she'd found it an intriguing puzzle. But to involve the police?

"I have an idea," Monica finally said. "I'm on fairly good terms with Detective Stevens. How about if I have an informal chat with her and see what she thinks?"

"Would you? That would be fantastic. I can't get over the idea that something doesn't seem quite right about Marta's death."

What had she gotten herself into? Monica thought when ended the call. She really hadn't wanted to get any more involved in this than she already was.

She sighed as she floured her work surface, dumped the raised dough out of the bowl and began to knead it. As she worked, the dough snapped and popped, slowly becoming more elastic and less sticky. The dough was studded with cranberries and a swirl of cinnamon, and before baking Monica would add a cinnamon and sugar topping.

She was so engrossed in what she was doing, she almost didn't hear the door open. She was surprised — Kit had taken the morning off and she didn't expect him until after lunch.

But it wasn't Kit, it was Lauren, Jeff's fiancée. She was bundled up against the cold in a dark green fur-trimmed parka and a chunky knitted cap, her blond hair streaming down her back.

"It smells so good in here," Lauren said as she pulled off her cap. "I'm starved."

"There are some muffins in that basket over there." Monica pointed to the counter. "Please help yourself."

"Thanks. I think I will."

Lauren reached for a muffin and took a bite. "Mmmm, delicious." She brushed some crumbs from the front of her jacket. "I have some good news for you."

"Oh?" Monica looked up from the dough she was arranging into loaf pans.

"The magazine *Michigan Today* wants to do an article on the Pepper Pot here in town. The owner told them about his new culinary creation, Sassamanash Farm Delight, and they want to include a little something about the farm and your cranberry compote."

"That's wonderful!" Monica peeled off her gloves. "That will be great exposure for us and the restaurant."

Lauren, who had graduated with a degree in marketing, often helped with public relations and marketing for the farm and Monica was very grateful for her help. It was time-consuming enough to do most of the baking herself along with the bookkeeping and accounting.

"Just let me know what I need to do," Monica said as she slid the loaves of bread into the oven. The blast of heat from the open oven door blew tendrils of hair around her face.

"I will. I'm meeting with the reporter later today."

Lauren continued to linger. It wasn't like her—she normally took on life at a trot, filling her plate with as many things as she could, working remotely for a firm in Chicago, doing freelance work when she could get it, as well as finding innovative ways to market Sassamanash Farm.

Lauren wet her lips. "Did Jeff tell you about that new therapy that might help his arm?" she said finally.

"Yes, he did."

Lauren raised her chin. "I think he should do it."

"He said it was very expensive."

"I know." Lauren fiddled with the zipper on her jacket. "But I think it would be worth it."

"I agree. But how would he be able to afford to pay for it? He said his insurance wouldn't cover the cost."

Lauren raised her chin. "I don't know. I'm sure we can find a way."

Monica thought over the conversation after Lauren had left. She had the distinct feeling that Lauren knew something that she wasn't telling her.

Monica finished the morning's baking, delivered the finished product to Nora at the farm store, and then realized she still hadn't done anything about contacting Detective Stevens to see when they could meet.

She decided to make the call when she got back to her cottage. She was getting hungry and it was time for lunch.

Mittens was on hand to greet her when she opened her back door. Monica picked the kitten up and spent a few minutes scratching under her chin and rubbing noses. Greg had headed off to Book 'Em, but the faint scent of his aftershave lingered in the kitchen. Monica took a deep breath and felt herself relax.

She retrieved some leftover pea soup—or *erwtensoep*, as the Dutch called it—from the refrigerator and put it on the stove to heat. The Dutch had settled Cranberry Cove in the eighteen hundreds, farmers and furniture makers by trade, and their influence had continued to the present day with many of the residents of Cranberry Cove being descendants of the original settlers.

Monica decided she would call Detective Stevens while her soup heated. She dialed Stevens's cell phone number but the call went to voice mail. Monica was about to dish out her soup when her phone rang. Stevens was returning her call.

Rather than meet at the police station, Stevens suggested they have a cup of coffee at the Cranberry Cove Diner—it would be more informal and more comfortable. And fewer tongues would wag, Monica thought. The townspeople were incredibly curious and loved to gossip, and they'd certainly want to know what she was doing if they caught her heading into the police station.

Monica finished her soup, put her bowl in the dishwasher, washed out the pan and left it to dry. She gave Mittens a scratch on the chin and headed out the door.

It was another clear day, and when she crested the hill leading into town, Cranberry Cove and Lake Michigan beyond were spread out in front of her. Closer to the shore, thick fingers of ice reached out into the twinkling water beyond. All the boats that normally bobbed in the horseshoe-shaped harbor were in dry dock and the parking lot of the Cranberry Cove Yacht Club was nearly empty.

As Monica headed down the hill, the microscopic pastel dots in the distance resolved themselves into the shops along Beach Hollow Road. She passed Gumdrops, where the identical twin VanVelsen sisters held court, drove past Danielle's Boutique and past Twilight, where Tempest Storm had arranged a display of crystals in the window that caught the light and reflected it back.

She couldn't believe her luck when she found a parking spot right in front of the Cranberry Cove Diner. It was a bit past lunchtime—the residents of Cranberry Cove generally awoke early and went to bed early—and not yet time for dinner, when workmen arrived in their overalls and work boots to eat simple dishes like open-faced turkey sandwiches and meat loaf and mashed potatoes.

Gus Armentas, the owner of the Cranberry Cove Diner and the short-order cook, nodded at Monica as she entered. Monica had gone from being new to Cranberry Cove and not worthy of Gus's notice to warranting a brief nod. Smiles were reserved for long-time residents and Monica had no idea how long it would be before she attained that status. Tourists to Cranberry Cove received a scowl when they entered, but that didn't deter them—the delicious smell of bacon frying lured them in anyway. The line to get in for breakfast was always out the door in the summertime.

Two people sat at the counter watching as Gus flipped a couple of burgers and lowered French fries into a vat of bubbling oil. A woman with impossibly red hair and obviously false eyelashes sat in one of the booths texting on her cell phone, pecking at the keys with long artificial nails. She wasn't a resident—Monica thought perhaps she was a realtor from out of town. The rest of the seats were empty.

Monica had just settled into a booth when Stevens arrived, pushing back the hood of her parka and stripping off her gloves.

Her look, when she slid into the seat opposite Monica, was one of curiosity.

"What have you gotten yourself involved in this time?" She smiled.

Monica took a deep breath. She felt somewhat ridiculous even bringing the matter up with Stevens, but she'd promised Dana.

She explained about Dana finding the receipt for the beta blocker pills and how the pills themselves were nowhere to be found in Marta's house.

They were quiet as the waitress placed two cups of coffee on the table. Some of the coffee sloshed over the side of the cup. Monica grabbed several napkins from the dispenser and soaked up the spilled liquid from the saucer.

Stevens reached for the sugar and added two packets to her cup.

"And you think that means something?" she said to Monica after stirring her coffee.

"I don't know. Dana—Marta's sister—thinks it does. Unfortunately there wasn't an autopsy."

Stevens nodded. "The ME ruled it death by natural causes." Stevens blew on her coffee and took a sip. "Is there a reason to doubt that? Other than those missing pills, and I'm not sure that's related."

"A big developer wanted to buy Marta's property for a very tempting sum of money. But Marta wasn't the sole owner of the property—it was left to her along with her brother John and sister Dana. They all had to agree to sell, and according to John, Marta refused."

Stevens raised her eyebrows. "Sounds like that could be a motive. Still . . ." She toyed with her spoon.

Monica hadn't decided whether or not she would tell Stevens about Dana's amnesia. It was possible it had nothing to do with the case. On the other hand, what if it did?

"There's another thing. Dana Bakker showed up at my door on Saturday night claiming someone was trying to kill her."

Stevens's jaw dropped. "What?" She dropped the spoon she had been playing with and it hit the table with a clatter.

"Why didn't she go to the police? What was she doing at your house?"

"She said she had amnesia and couldn't remember what had happened before the accident that sent her to the hospital. She was here in Cranberry Cove looking for the house she remembered being at—one of the only things she could remember." Monica ran her finger around the rim of her coffee cup. "Her car skidded off the road and ended up moored in a snowbank."

Stevens frowned. "What was she doing at your place? Unless she was coming to see you?"

Monica shook her head. "It was dark, and she said she turned down the street to our cottage by accident, having gotten confused as to where she was."

"What was this accident she claimed to have had?" Stevens took a sip of her coffee and momentarily closed her eyes.

Monica explained about the accident and how Dana was convinced she'd been fleeing someone.

Stevens pinched the bridge of her nose. "That certainly changes things, although I'm not sure how. It would be quite convenient for Dana to claim amnesia if she'd killed her sister herself."

"So you do think it's possible that Marta was murdered and didn't die of natural causes?"

Stevens held up a hand. "Whoa, I wouldn't go that far. But I do agree there are some questions. Some very curious questions." She picked up her coffee cup. "Have they had the funeral yet?"

"No. At least not that I know of."

"I'll see if I can get an order approved for an autopsy. I can't make any promises—the county doesn't like spending any more money than it has to—but I'll do my best."

• • •

Monica felt conflicted when she left the diner. She'd felt obligated to tell Stevens about Dana but at the same time she felt slightly guilty for doing it, as if she had betrayed Dana's confidence somehow.

She shrugged her feelings off as she headed down the street to Gumdrops, the pastel pink candy store next to Danielle's. She stopped in front of the boutique's window for a moment to admire the beautiful mohair coat on display. It wasn't something she would ever need—her life was all about jeans and sweatshirts for working and her black pants and silk blouse for occasions that might warrant something dressier.

Hennie VanVelsen was in the window of Gumdrops rearranging a display of packages of salty black licorice, a much-beloved Dutch treat, and boxes of Droste chocolate pastilles.

She smiled broadly when Monica entered the shop.

"How are you, dear? It's been a while. Keeping busy at the farm, are you?"

Gerda came out from behind the counter to join them. She and her twin were wearing identical pale blue skirts and cardigans, and even though Monica had known them for a while now, she still had trouble telling them apart.

"What can we get for you today, dear?" Hennie said.

"Some Wilhelmina mints perhaps?"

Monica knew her stepmother, Gina, enjoyed them, and it gave her an excuse to talk to the VanVelsens, who loved to gossip and were the unofficial town historians.

Hennie reached for a tin of the peppermints with the silhouette of Princess Wilhelmina on the front.

"You didn't by any chance happen to know Marta Kuiper, did you?"

Hennie looked almost affronted. "Of course we did." She patted the marcel waves in her silver hair. "I was sorry to hear that she was gone. Marta was the niece of a dear friend of ours who also sadly passed away two years ago."

"Such a strange girl," Gerda piped up.

"Oh?"

Monica knew she didn't have to say much to keep the conversation going—the floodgates were open.

Hennie nodded. "She tended to keep to herself."

This time Gerda nodded. "Shy and reclusive, you could say. Even as a young girl. Although it got worse as she got older."

Hennie's mouth curled down. "Her brother took advantage of that, if you ask me. He and his sister went off and left Marta to care for their mother, the poor thing."

"Marta claimed she didn't mind, but what kind of a life was that? Stuck in that old house. Their father was as stingy as they come and refused to spend any money for repairs or modernization. Now, I believe in thrift—all the Dutch do—but he took it too far." Gerda smoothed the front of her ruffled blouse.

"And still there wasn't all that much money left after he passed," Hennie said. "Everyone was quite surprised."

"Had you stayed in touch with Marta?" Monica asked.

"We tried to," Hennie said. "It's what our friend would have wanted. We invited her for dinner occasionally or we went to her place for tea." Hennie picked a bit of lint off her sweater. "We hated to think of her living in that house alone without any company."

"She did have that cousin of hers living there though," Gerda said.

"Yes, of course." Hennie looked slightly irritated. "Cheryl DeSantis. I'd forgotten about her."

"Was she still living with Marta, do you know?" Monica asked.

It hadn't looked to her as if anybody else had been occupying the house.

"No, I don't think so. We were there just the other day and didn't see her," Gerda said. "It's so hard to believe the poor thing is gone."

"What day was that?" Monica said, her excitement rising.

"It was Friday, wasn't it, Hennie?"

Hennie nodded. "Yes, it was Friday. I remember because that's one of the days we have a girl come in to help us in the shop. We usually take the afternoon off to go to the beauty parlor or to visit the cemetery and our dear parents' grave."

"On the way back from the cemetery we passed Marta's house and decided to stop in," Gerda said.

"We didn't stay long." Hennie's mouth turned down again. "We were having a nice visit and cup of tea with Marta and her friend Joyce when Marta's brother arrived." Hennie shuddered. "I never could stand the man. Even as a young boy he was arrogant and pushy. Of course, he was very smart and went on to become a surgeon."

"He said he had important things to discuss with Marta, so we had to leave," Gerda said. "He practically threw us out."

Hennie gave Gerda a stern look. "I wouldn't go that far."

Gerda ignored her sister. "Then as we were leaving, Marta's sister, Dana, arrived. She was the youngest and we never really knew her all that well. She was a polite little girl, very studious. I think she moved to the other side of the state."

"Sounds like some kind of family powwow," Monica said.

"I should imagine." Hennie fingered the cameo pin at the neck of her blouse. "They hardly ever visited Marta. And John did say they had important matters to discuss."

Monica thought she had a good idea of what it was that John wanted to discuss with Marta and Dana—the offer from the developer to buy their land. Had that discussion led to murder?

• • •

Monica decided to walk down to Making Scents, Gina's shop, and give her the peppermints since she hadn't seen her for a few days. Gina had arrived in Cranberry Cove from Chicago in all her finery — fancy car, leather pants and expensively highlighted hair — and had decided to stay to be near her son. Monica's father had left her mother for Gina and had subsequently left Gina for a younger model. The three women had created a cordial alliance, sharing their heartbreak and giving each other support.

Somehow Gina, who had been extremely high-maintenance, had managed to adapt to life in a pokey little town where the local beauty parlor still boasted hooded hair dryers, and had opened a shop selling essential oils. Everyone had been surprised when she'd survived her first year in business and had slowly built a loyal clientele. Tourists loved her shop, and her, and stocked up while they were in town for the summer or the autumn leaf tours, and even some of the locals had come around to the idea of aromatherapy.

Monica left Gumdrops and picked her way down the side-walk — there were still patches of ice here and there despite the merchants having scattered plenty of salt in an attempt to melt it.

She passed the Cranberry Cove Diner, and even though she wasn't in the least bit hungry, the smell of frying bacon made her mouth water. She popped into Greg's shop, Book 'Em, for a brief hello and a quick kiss and then continued down Beach Hollow Road.

The lake, visible in the distance, was the color of steel and made Monica shiver when she looked at it.

Gina's shop was next to the hardware store. She had added a jaunty blue and white awning to dress up the front and bottles of essential oils were carefully arranged in the window. *Making Scents* was spelled out in elegant gold letters above the window.

Monica was surprised to see a large bin sitting next to the front door.

A bell tinkled melodically when Monica pushed open the door. The air was perfumed with the mingled scents of lavender, mint and eucalyptus.

Gina was teetering on a chair, swiping a feather duster at the elaborate crystal chandelier hanging in the middle of the shop.

"Careful," Monica said, holding out a hand as Gina jumped down.

The one thing Gina hadn't done was bow to the sartorial customs of Cranberry Cove, which generally included jeans or work pants, warm sweaters in the winter and T-shirts in the summer.

Gina was wearing leopard-print leggings, a black velvet tunic with a V-neck, high-heeled, open-toed suede booties and a pendant on a long silver chain that looked as if it had probably come from Tempest Storm's shop, Twilight.

"I've brought you a present," Monica said, holding out the paper bag from Gumdrops.

Gina peered inside. "Why, thank you. You know I love these. That's sweet of you." Gina opened the tin and offered it to Monica.

"Why is that bin outside your front door?" Monica said as she helped herself to a mint.

"That's for our food drive. I'll be putting a sign on it as soon as they arrive from the print shop. All the merchants are participating. You'll soon be seeing similar bins up and down the street."

"What are you collecting the food for?"

"The local food pantry. January and February are difficult months for them. Everyone donates during the holidays—from Thanksgiving to Christmas they are usually well stocked. But donations fall off as soon as the new year starts."

Gina fiddled with some bottles on a mirrored tray on the counter. "I couldn't bear the thought of people not having enough to eat so I decided to organize a food drive."

"It's a wonderful idea," Monica said. "I'd be glad to do my part. I can donate some breads and muffins."

Gina pursed her lips. "It might be best if you take those directly to the food pantry. We have volunteers collecting the food from the bins outside everyone's shop, but I don't know how often they will be doing that."

Gina went behind the counter and leaned her elbows on it. "I've been in kind of a slump lately to be honest with you. Frankly, my romantic life is nonexistent." Gina pouted. "There are no eligible men here." She rolled her eyes. "You were lucky to nab Greg Harper when you did."

Monica didn't think she'd *nabbed* Greg exactly. She'd hardly set a snare for him like some sort of Venus flytrap. As a matter of fact, romance had been the last thing on her mind as they had gotten to know each other over time.

"But I did see something hopeful this morning." Gina leaned forward and her necklace clanged against the counter. She lowered her voice to a throaty whisper. "A gorgeous Jaguar came down Beach Hollow Road—and I'm not talking about the animal—and parked right in front of the hardware store next door. I got a brief glimpse of the driver when he got out of the car—tall and slim with thick silver hair." She winked at Monica. "And decidedly male."

Gina frowned. "I had a couple of customers in the shop so I couldn't go introduce myself, but I'm hopeful I can track him down before someone else grabs him." She rolled her eyes. "Not that there's a lot of competition in this town. That's one good thing at least."

Monica froze. It sounded like Gina had seen John Kuiper in town. Jaguars didn't prowl the streets of Cranberry Cove often, not even among the tourists who flooded the town in good weather. Monica didn't want to be the one to tell Gina that John already had a trophy wife who was probably at least twenty years Gina's junior. It was unlikely that John would be spending much more time in Cranberry Cove anyway. Gina would soon give up and be onto something else.

Gina was silent for a moment. She tilted her head to the side. "You wouldn't happen to know who that man is, would you?"

Monica opened her mouth but nothing came out. She shook her head quickly.

"Nope. Never seen him before." She hoped that didn't sound as insincere as it felt.

Gina gave a gusty sigh. "I so wish I could have what you and Greg have."

Monica wanted to tell her that she needed to stop going after the wrong sort of men—the ones with lots of money, big houses and fast cars. If she would settle for someone normal, she might be able to have the love she wanted.

• • •

Monica made a stop at Bart's Butcher Shop and purchased pork chops for dinner. She planned to cook them with cranberries, shallots and a bit of balsamic vinegar. It was one of Greg's favorite meals.

By the time she got back to the cottage, Greg's car was already in the driveway.

"You're home early," Monica said as she put her packages down on the kitchen table.

Greg was unpacking a box he'd placed on the counter. He indicated it with a nod of his head.

"I went to an estate sale this afternoon. I was beginning to think I had wasted my time when I found a first edition Ngaio Marsh—*A Man Lay Dead*—published in 1934, the first book in her Roderick Alleyn series. It was like finding a pearl in an oyster. It's in mint condition, too. It doesn't look like it had ever even been cracked open. I also picked up some current best sellers. Customers are always looking for those at a reduced price."

Monica opened the refrigerator and paused with her hand on the handle. She had a sudden thought.

"I can't remember if I turned the oven off in the farm kitchen."

Greg looked over his shoulder at her. "You probably did it by rote. It's one of those things you don't think about—you just do it. Then later you can't remember actually doing it."

Monica bit her lip. "I don't know. I think I'd better check."

She took her jacket from the coatrack and slipped it back on. "I'll be right back," she said as she headed out the back door.

The sun was getting lower in the sky and it felt as if the temperature had dropped even lower. Monica hadn't bothered to grab her hat or gloves. She turned up the collar on her jacket and stuck her hands in her pockets.

The last few rays of sun glinted off the ice covering the cranberry bogs. There were small paw prints in the snow—a fox perhaps?

The wind shifted slightly and it whistled down her back. She quickened her steps.

Finally the building was in sight. A light was burning in one of the windows. Had she forgotten to turn those off, too?

Monica fumbled in her pocket for the key, her fingers clumsy and numb from the cold.

She finally got the door open and stepped inside. She was walking toward the oven when she heard a noise. It sounded as if it was coming from the storage room at the back of the kitchen. She prayed it wasn't a mouse—it might chew through the bags of flour and sugar kept in there. That had happened once already and the mess had nearly made Monica cry.

She hurried across the kitchen and was about to reach for the door to the storage room when it opened. She couldn't help it—she was so startled she screamed.

She wasn't sure who was more surprised to see the other, her or Kit.

"I didn't know you were still here," Monica said somewhat breathlessly. Her heart was beating so hard she could hear it thudding in her ears.

"I didn't expect you to come back," Kit said, glancing behind him.

"I came to make sure I'd turned off the oven. Then I thought I heard a mouse."

Monica peered into the storage room. There was something spread out on the floor. It looked like a sleeping bag.

A sheepish look came over Kit's face.

"Have you been sleeping here at night?" Monica said.

"It's only temporary, darling." Kit looked at his feet. "I didn't think you'd mind."

"But don't you and Sean have a house?"

"Yes, of course. But there's been a tiny problem, you see. Sean and I had this itsy-bitsy little tiff. Nothing serious. I'm sure it will blow over. But at the moment we're not speaking to each other."

"Well, I certainly don't mind if you stay here, but I hate to think of you sleeping on the floor."

"I don't mind in the least." Kit put a hand on his hip. "I'm tougher than I look, you know, darling."

• • •

Monica finished rearranging the muffins and scones on the assortment of trays she'd collected for use at the farm store and brushed some flour from the front of her sweatshirt. The trays of baked goods were going to the store for sale and she had another box filled with what she planned to take to the food pantry.

"That really is terribly good of you, darling," Kit said as he helped Monica carry the boxes to her car. "I'm sure people will appreciate having something fresh to eat. Food pantries are usually all boxes of hamburger helper and dented cans of beans."

Monica started the car, waved to Kit and headed downtown. She felt a glow of satisfaction as she drove. It was a good feeling to be doing something for others—it was easy to forget that there were people in need when you were wrapped up in work and your own daily life.

The food pantry was located across the drawbridge that spanned the inlet into the harbor. It was down a street so narrow and dark it could have been mistaken for an alley and was located right next to Flynn's, a rough bar for hard drinkers that was known for the fights that broke out nearly every night.

It was a tight squeeze, but Monica maneuvered her Focus around the turn and down the narrow space. She found a parking spot at the bottom of the hill not too far from the food pantry and parked the car.

She stacked the boxes of baked goods and managed to carry them to the food pantry in one trip. She placed them on the counter with a sigh of relief.

The waiting room was nearly full with people patiently waiting their turn to select food from the nearly bare shelves behind the counter.

A woman was at the counter holding a bag of canned goods that Monica assumed she was dropping off. She smelled of tobacco and looked slightly disheveled, as if she'd rolled out of bed moments earlier and into whatever clothes were at hand. Although she appeared to be in her forties and must have once been quite attractive, there were deep lines running between her nose and mouth and her face was puffy.

She was talking to the food pantry volunteer, and Monica couldn't help overhearing their conversation.

"I'm sorry about your cousin Marta," the volunteer said. Her name tag read *Dorothy*. "She was always a great help to us. We're going to miss her."

"Marta Kuiper?" Monica said as she edged closer. "She was your cousin?"

The woman turned toward Monica. "Did you know her?" Her voice was husky, from cigarettes, Monica guessed.

"Not exactly. I know her sister, Dana."

"Cheryl DeSantis," the woman said, holding out her hand. Several bangle bracelets on her wrist jangled melodically.

"I'm sorry for your loss," Monica said. "Were you and Marta close?"

Cheryl sniffed. "Yes, we were. Marta was so good to me. She let me move in with her when I was . . . uh . . . between houses." She smiled. "She wanted me to stay, but I didn't want to take advantage of her generosity—it was so kind of her—plus, I had made other arrangements. It was time for me to move on." She leaned closer and the smell of cigarettes and whiskey on her breath drifted toward Monica. "I wanted my own place." She gave a pained smile. "You know how it is."

Monica nodded.

"It was nice to meet you," Cheryl said as she picked up the bag of canned goods and turned to leave. "I have to go."

So she had been wrong, Monica thought. Cheryl was getting food from the food pantry, not donating. If Cheryl had hit hard times, she wondered why she didn't move back in with Marta. Was it pride?

Of course, she might have a low-income apartment and simply needed help with food. Many people were living from paycheck to paycheck and often came up short at the end of the week and couldn't even afford a box of macaroni and cheese or a packet of ramen noodles.

Dorothy beamed when she saw Monica's box of baked goods.

"These will be so appreciated. You can't even imagine," she said. "We never get anything fresh, although in the summer we occasionally have farmers donate vegetables and fruit. But the winters can be grim—all processed food."

Monica was glad she had decided to donate. She and Dorothy chatted for a few minutes and then Monica left.

Cheryl was still outside on the sidewalk putting her bag of canned goods into the backseat of her car. The car was old and rust had eaten away at the wheel wells. It looked to be on its last legs. The backseat was filled with what looked like Cheryl's possessions—clothes, shoes, bags of potato chips and other junk food.

Was she living out of her car? Monica wondered. Then why on earth would she turn down Marta's offer to live with her?

Or was there more to it than Cheryl had admitted?

Monica watched, curious, as Cheryl walked up the street toward Flynn's, pulled open the door and went inside.

Chapter 7

Monica drove back down Beach Hollow Road toward Sassamanash Farm. The lake, in the distance, looked cold and forbidding and the wind, which was blowing dark clouds in from the west, was buffeting Monica's small car. She hoped more snow wasn't on the way. The winter had already seemed to be decades long.

She couldn't wait for spring, when things would begin to bloom—the pink flowers on the cranberry vines, the climbing roses on the trellis outside her back door, the fragrant herbs in her small garden.

She was rounding a bend in the road near the farm when she noticed a car stopped by the side of the road and a woman standing next to it.

As Monica got closer she realized the woman was Joyce Murphy, Marta's friend. She slowed and pulled over onto the shoulder opposite Joyce's station wagon. Monica checked the traffic, carefully opened her door and got out of the car.

She crunched along the snow piled on the shoulder of the road, at one point nearly slipping on a patch of black ice. A frigid wind blew in off the lake and she huddled in her parka as she dashed across the street.

Joyce had her arms wrapped around herself as she stood waiting in the cold beside her car.

"What's happened?" Monica asked when she was within earshot. "Have you had a breakdown?"

"I don't know. I had the car at the garage for a tune-up just the other week—Smitty's right outside of town. I've been going there for years. I think it must be the battery. The nice young man who looked after me warned me that I'd soon need a new one but I didn't want to spend the money until I had to." She sighed. "Penny wise and pound foolish, as my dear mother used to say."

"Have you called for a tow truck?" Monica shouted over the roar of the wind blowing in off the lake.

Joyce shook her head. "No. I'm afraid I forgot to bring my cell phone with me."

Monica noticed Joyce's car was filled with cardboard boxes of canned goods. "Were you headed to the food pantry with that?" she asked. She was puzzled since the food pantry was in the opposite direction.

"Yes, but I was going to go home for a bite of lunch first. I was feeling a bit wobbly, I'm afraid. I'm one of the volunteers who are collecting the donations from all the merchants in town. I'm pleased to say we've done quite well, as you can see."

"You must be frozen solid standing out here," Monica said. "That wind is bitter. Why don't we sit in my car and call the towing company?"

They waited till a truck had zoomed past them, sending slush and snow flying in its wake, then made their way across the street. Joyce sighed as they settled in the warmth of Monica's car.

Monica retrieved her cell phone from her pocket and dialed the local towing company. She knew the number by heart—her ancient Ford Focus had broken down numerous times and she knew she'd soon have to face the fact that she'd need to replace it.

"It seems they're quite busy," Monica said after ending the call. "It's going to be over an hour before they can get here."

"I couldn't possibly ask you to wait that long," Joyce said, her hand already on the door handle.

"Why don't we go back to my house? I've got some leftover beef and barley soup in the fridge. We could do with something to warm us up."

Joyce's face lit up. "That does sound heavenly," she said, settling back in her seat.

Monica put the car in gear and headed down the road, quickly traversing the short distance to Sassamanash Farm.

"What a darling place," Joyce said, clasping her hands together when Monica's cottage came into view and they made their way down the drive to the farm.

"Come on in." Monica held the back door open for Joyce. "Don't mind Mittens. She's very friendly."

Mittens stared at the visitor curiously then began to walk in and out between Monica's legs, her long tail swishing back and forth, nearly tripping her.

"I'll get the soup going," Monica said as she led the way to the kitchen. "Take the chair over there by the heating vent and get warm."

"This is so kind of you, dear." Joyce kicked off her boots and hung her coat from the back of the chair. She sat down with a sigh of relief.

"How long had you and Marta been friends?" Monica asked as she got the container of soup from the refrigerator and poured it into a pot.

"We go way back," Joyce said, folding her hands and putting them on the table. "All the way back to elementary school. Marta's family has been here in Cranberry Cove for generations. My family moved here when I was seven years old. My father took a job with the Baker Furniture Company. It was hard adapting to a new school and a new place. Before that we'd lived in Iowa, you see. It's so terribly flat there that the hills and valleys here took me quite by surprise."

Monica got bowls out of the cupboard and two spoons out of the drawer.

"Can I do something to help, dear?"

"Thank you, but there's no need. You sit and rest. I hope you're getting warm."

"Delightfully so. It's those small pleasures that are so important in life," Joyce said. "Getting warm when you've been cold, eating when you're hungry. Who needs the grand things in life when all your needs are being met?"

Joyce had a point, Monica thought.

"That very first day at my new school I was scared half to death," Joyce continued. "I remember my knees were shaking when my mother dropped me off outside the second-grade classroom." Joyce's eyes took on a faraway look. "But Marta befriended me almost immediately. Later on I realized how unusual that was—she was painfully shy and didn't really mingle much with the other children. Perhaps she sensed a kindred spirit in me that day."

"How wonderful to have had such a long friendship," Monica said as she ladled the hot soup into bowls. Steam rose up from the hot liquid and bathed her face.

"Yes, we were certainly blessed." Joyce gave a sniff and fumbled in her purse for a tissue. "I'm certainly going to miss her. I was quite alarmed when I thought she'd be moving."

"Oh?" Monica put the bowls on the table.

"Yes. When the developer made that offer for her land. It was an incredible amount of money for someone like Marta, who had spent her life scrimping and saving and making do."

"But I understand she didn't plan to sell."

"She didn't. Money can't buy everything, you see. She'd grown up in that house. It was all she'd ever known and she didn't want to leave no matter what her brother did."

"John?" Monica's ears perked up. "What did John do?"

"He was putting pressure on her. He wouldn't let up. He had the poor thing in tears at times. He even put her name down on a waiting list at the Sunnyside Retirement Community in Grand Rapids. As if Marta wanted to move that far away from everything and everyone she knew."

"Why would John do that?" Monica asked even though she knew the answer.

"For the money, of course. He stood to inherit a third of the profits."

"I thought John was quite successful. Dana says he's a surgeon. I've always heard they make a lot of money."

Joyce looked at her slyly and tapped the side of her nose. "Things aren't always what they seem, are they?" she said cryptically.

• • •

Monica was pulling a sheet of cranberry walnut chocolate chip cookies from the oven when she had an idea. She would put together a snack for Jeff, some cookies and a flask of hot coffee. He was out on the bogs laying down sand and would probably appreciate something to eat.

She brewed some coffee, steam wreathing her face as she poured it into a thermos, placed several of the warm cookies in a bag and headed out.

Jeff was out on a tractor at the far end of the bog nearest the farm kitchen. The bog was covered in a thick layer of opaque ice. Jeff had already spread a layer of sand over half of the bog. He was heading away from Monica, and when he turned she waved to him.

He swung the tractor around and drove over to where Monica was standing.

"I've brought you some hot coffee and cookies fresh from the oven. I thought you might be able to use a snack."

Jeff's face lit up. It was ruddy from the cold, his cheeks and the tip of his nose bright red. "How did you know I was beginning to get hungry? You're a lifesaver, Sis." He opened the bag of cookies and sniffed deeply. "These smell delicious."

Monica unscrewed the cap to the thermos and poured him some coffee. "This should warm you up."

Monica held the cookies while Jeff cupped a hand around the coffee and took a sip.

He sighed. "Just what I needed." He handed the cup back to Monica. "I'll take the cookies on the tractor with me." He squinted at the sky. "I need to get this done before the sun goes down. There's snow in the forecast for tomorrow."

Monica was walking back to the farm kitchen when her cell phone rang. She pulled it from her pocket and glanced at the number. It was Gina.

"Hello?"

"Monica? This is Gina. I found something you should probably see," Gina said somewhat enigmatically. "I think it might relate to the death of that woman you were telling me about."

• • •

Monica closed up the farm kitchen, got into her Focus and headed back toward town, her curiosity decidedly piqued by Gina's call. What on earth could Gina have found that related to Marta's death?

She parked in front of the Purple Grape, the Cranberry Cove wine store that was mostly frequented by summer visitors. The local residents were more concerned with the price of a bottle of wine than its vintage and tended to go in for the boxed stuff sold at the large chain grocery store just outside of town.

The sun was starting to go down and although the sky was still bright, the shadows were deepening. The large ceramic flowerpots outside the shops that overflowed with flowers in the summer were now topped with snow and snow was banked along the sides of the road where the plows had pushed it.

Monica passed Bijou, the jewelry store, where a few pieces were displayed in the window — a strand of pearls, a gold watch and a silver charm bracelet.

She crossed the street to Gina's shop, picking her way through the slush that had accumulated along the curb. A customer was at the counter waiting while Gina rang up several bottles of essential oils. Monica pretended to study a display of books on aromatherapy while she waited.

Finally the customer left and the shop was empty. Monica went over to the counter and leaned on it.

"So what did you find? I have to say, I was terribly intrigued by your telephone call."

Gina took a rag from under the counter and scrubbed at a spot on the glass. "I wouldn't have thought much of anything about it if it hadn't been for that woman's death and the bottle of missing pills you told me about. When we put out the food collection bins, I suspected that at some point someone was going to decide to use one of them as a trash can." Gina rolled her eyes. "And I was right. People can be so lazy. They can't be bothered to walk to the end of the block and dispose of their garbage appropriately."

Gina reached under the counter again. "I found this in our bin." She put a prescription pill bottle on the counter. "Someone must have dropped it in there instead of in the trash can. I guess it was too far to walk."

Monica picked up the pill bottle. Could it be . . . ?

The corner of the label was missing, but it was still easy enough to read. The bottle had been issued to Marta Kuiper and contained a thirty-day supply of atenolol — a generic beta blocker. And it was empty.

Monica held it up. "There weren't any pills in here?"

"No." Gina shook her head. "I only happened to find it because I accidentally dropped my keys in the bin when I was locking the door and had to fish them out." Gina pointed to the bottle. "Do you think it means anything?"

"I don't know." Monica bit her lip. "I think it might. I guess I'll leave it up to Detective Stevens to decide."

• • •

Detective Stevens furrowed her brow and tapped the pill bottle on her desk in a slow rhythm.

Monica waited patiently. She was seated across from Stevens's desk in her office at the police station. The chair was rather hard and she squirmed around trying to get comfortable.

Stevens's desk was awash with papers, some in labeled folders, many with coffee rings on top, and others loose. A chipped and stained coffee mug was next to her laptop and a piece of aluminum foil was balled up next to it. The remains of a stale doughnut sat on a napkin on top of one of the stacks of paper.

Stevens tapped the pill bottle against her chin. She let out a heavy sigh.

"I don't know. You said you found this in one of the food collection bins?"

"Yes. Or rather my stepmother, Gina, did. It was in the bin in front of her shop Making Scents."

"I'm trying to decide if there's any real significance in the fact that this bottle"—she waved it toward Monica—"is empty. It's possible that Marta Kuiper took the pills out of the bottle and put them somewhere else." She looked at Monica. "You did say she used a pill caddy, didn't you?"

"Yes, but it only holds enough pills for the week. That prescription is for a thirty-day supply."

"Still. Why throw it in one of the collection bins? Why not the trash?"

"I don't know."

"If your suspicions are correct," Stevens continued, "that someone gave Marta Kuiper an overdose of these pills, that would make it . . . murder."

Monica nodded. "Yes."

Stevens's shoulders rose up and down as she sighed again. "I'll see what I can do. They still haven't held the burial yet, have they?"

"No. I believe it's scheduled for tomorrow."

"I'm still trying to get the county to agree to an autopsy. But I can't make any promises." Stevens frowned. "If the body has already been embalmed — which I imagine it has — we won't be able to get an accurate toxicology report. But if there's anything else out of the ordinary, the pathologist will find it."

Chapter 8

Monica was setting the table and Greg was ensconced in a chair by the fire with the newspaper when she heard a car coming down the drive.

That was odd — it was an unusual time for a visit. Most people were in the midst of preparing dinner, eating it, or already cleaning up from it if they were early diners.

Monica peered out the back door window as the car came into view. She recognized Dana's fancy BMW.

She turned down the water she was boiling for the pasta she was planning to cook for dinner and waited for a knock on the door.

Dana's expression, when Monica opened the door, clearly showed that something was wrong. Her mouth was set in a tight line and her eyebrows were drawn together in a frown.

She was wearing boots this time — Monica recognized them from a display in Danielle's window.

"I'm sorry for disturbing you," she said as she wiped her feet on the mat. "Do you mind if I come in?"

Monica held the door wider and showed Dana into the living room. Greg jumped to his feet, the newspaper sliding off his lap and onto the floor in a heap.

"I am interrupting you, I'm afraid," Dana said but made no move to leave. She perched on the edge of a chair.

"Has something happened?" Monica asked, noting the look of distress on Dana's face.

"John is in a terrible state, yelling and screaming. He's absolutely furious." Dana shuddered.

"Why? What's wrong?"

"You know Marta's service and burial were scheduled for tomorrow? The police called to say we have to postpone it. They are waiting for permission to do an autopsy on the body after all."

Greg cleared his throat. "Why don't I make you a cup of tea?" he said to Dana.

She nodded. "Thank you."

They were quiet for a moment, listening to the fire crackle and snap in the hearth. They could hear Greg filling the teakettle in the kitchen.

"Why are the police doing an autopsy?" Dana said finally, twisting her gloves around and around in her hands. "Everything was all set. John is absolutely furious. His face went all red when he heard and I was afraid he would have a stroke."

Greg returned with a mug of tea. "Sugar, no cream, if I remember correctly." He smiled and put the mug on the table next to Dana's chair.

"I can't understand why they're doing an autopsy at this late date. It's horribly inconvenient." Dana picked up the mug. "I was hoping to go back to East Lansing right after the burial." She shivered. "I don't feel safe here. I may not remember everything, but I do know someone was trying to kill me. How do I know they're not going to try again?"

"You don't remember anything new?" Monica said.

Dana pursed her lips. "Not really. Only the sensation of being in danger and of being pursued. I'm sure that's why I was driving the way they claim I was and why I had the accident." She studied her hands.

"You say you remember the feeling of being in danger—"

"Yes. Nothing specific, I'm afraid. Although I have had a flash of someone trying to hit me over the head with something." She looked away from Monica, out the window. "I've been having nightmares about it. I keep thinking I hear someone trying to break into the house." She shivered. "It's a dismal place. I don't know how poor Marta could stand it. I can't wait to get out of there."

She looked at Monica, her eyes pleading.

"I can understand how you feel. But the police are doing the autopsy because they've found some new evidence," Monica said.

Dana's hand jerked and she knocked her mug against the table. "New evidence? What new evidence?"

Monica couldn't help but notice the look of fear in Dana's eyes.

What was she afraid of? Monica wondered. Had she killed Marta herself and blocked out the memory?

And was her brother angry that the funeral and burial had been delayed or was he angry that the police were planning to perform an autopsy that might possibly reveal something damaging to him?

• • •

Kit was at the farm kitchen looking rumpled and bleary-eyed when Monica got there. The door to the storage room was open and she noticed his sleeping bag spread out on the floor. Obviously he'd spent another night bunking on the floor.

"You look like you could use some coffee," Monica said after saying good morning.

Kit ran his hand through his hair, rumpling it further. "You could say that."

"Why don't I put some on then."

"That's okay. I'll do it." Kit turned away and Monica got the sense that he was glad of the distraction.

Monica tied on her apron and began measuring out flour and sugar for the first batches of cranberry muffins. She was getting butter out of the refrigerator to soften when Kit handed her a steaming cup of coffee.

"This smells heavenly." Monica took a sip.

She was worried about Kit. His usual ebullient personality was diminished, like a light that had been dimmed. Surely he and Sean had made up by now? Kit was so good-natured, Monica couldn't imagine his staying angry for long.

"Don't tell me you and Sean haven't made up yet?" she said.

Kit looked stricken. His shoulders slumped and his mouth turned down. He held his hands out, palms up.

"We have. There's just one problem."

"Oh? What's that?"

"The argument we got into was over a bad investment Sean had made, one he hadn't told me about." Kit gulped and his Adam's apple bobbed up and down. "And now I'm afraid we've lost our house."

"What?" Monica was so startled she nearly dropped her mug. "But how?"

Kit shrugged. "Sean got this stock tip from a friend. Several actually. It was supposed to be foolproof. Guaranteed to earn us money." He rolled his eyes. "Sean used all our money to buy the shares. Instead of making money, we lost all of our savings. And on top of that, Sean's been laid off from his job."

"Oh, no." Monica knew how tenuous people's financial circumstances could be. More than once since she'd arrived, Sassamanash Farm had been skating on particularly thin ice. Several times Jeff had been convinced the farm was going to go under but somehow they had always pulled through.

"So you have nowhere to live?" Monica asked in disbelief.

"Not at the moment, although we did come into some luck. And it's about time." He tossed his head. "Sean has managed to lease a small apartment above Twilight, Tempest Storm's shop on Beach Hollow Road. But we won't be able to move in for a few days." Kit reached for his apron and tied it on. "Sean is bunking with a friend." He curled his lip. "I'm afraid this friend of his isn't a fan of me. I think he and Sean might have been romantically involved at one time, although far be it from me to ask questions." He pretended to lock his lips. "I decided it would be a good idea for me to camp out here instead." He made an exaggerated sad face.

"I'm really sorry to hear that. I hate to think of you here all night. Why don't you come up to the cottage and stay in our guest room?"

"You're a sweetheart, you really are," Kit said. "But this is fine as long as it's temporary. Please don't worry, darling. It will give you wrinkles."

• • •

Monica took the last tray of cranberry walnut chocolate chip cookies out of the oven. She'd been so distracted by thoughts of Marta's death, Dana and autopsies, that she'd burned the previous batch slightly.

She sighed. It wasn't the first time she'd done that and it wouldn't be the last. The cookies couldn't be sold — she prided herself on the quality of all of Sassamanash Farm's products — although they were still edible. She'd save them for Jeff and his crew. They were always happy to eat her missteps or her experiments that didn't quite work out.

She'd once tried to create a cranberry-based pudding that had sadly been a dismal failure, which she couldn't pawn off on anyone — including Jeff's workers.

Monica was transferring the cookies to cooling racks when her cell phone rang.

"Hello?"

"Monica? This is Tammy Stevens. I wanted to let you know that an autopsy was performed earlier on Marta Kuiper."

"Can you share the results? Did they find anything new?" Monica held her breath. She knew Stevens wasn't always at liberty to reveal information during the course of an investigation.

She heard Stevens sigh.

"We'll be releasing the information to the papers tomorrow, so I suppose it won't hurt to share it with you now."

Stevens cleared her throat, and Monica heard papers rustling.

"As I suspected, the body had been embalmed, making a tox screen unreliable. The pathologist performed one anyway, but we don't have those results back yet. The pathologist was able to determine one thing though."

Monica held her breath. She hoped the results indicated natural causes—that would put Dana's mind at rest, assuming she could be convinced of it.

Stevens continued. "It seems the pathologist discovered signs that Marta had been smothered."

Monica stifled a gasp.

"The ME was in such a hurry that he missed the signs, but the pathologist who is filling in for him while he's at that conference in Arizona basking in the sun did notice the signs. Granted, they were subtle. If you're right about the beta blockers, an overdose would have slowed her heart rate and her breathing, making it much easier for someone to smother her. They wouldn't have needed much strength at all, and she probably wouldn't have even been able to put up much of a fight."

• • •

Monica was greeted with delicious smells when she opened the door to her cottage. She'd put a pot roast in her slow cooker that morning and the aroma was heavenly enough to make her mouth water.

Mittens was on hand to greet her too, meowing loudly to indicate that it was time for dinner.

Monica retrieved a can of cat food from the cupboard and, with the cat winding in and out between her legs, managed to open it and spoon it out into Mittens's bowl.

Mittens gave a satisfactory *meow* before digging into the meal.

The back door opened, ushering in a blast of frigid air. The wind blew fresh snow across the threshold to the kitchen.

"Is it snowing?" Monica asked, turning her head for a kiss.

Greg's lips were cold and his hands on her cheeks were even colder. "Yes. It's started up again, I'm afraid, but it doesn't look like it will last."

"Famous last words," Monica said. "Jeff will be busy plowing tonight, I guess." Monica took some potatoes from a basket in the pantry, rummaged in a drawer she had vowed a million times to clean out until she found her peeler, and began to peel the potatoes to add to the slow cooker now that the meat was nearly done.

"Do you think the snow is going to stick?" she asked.

Greg shrugged. "I don't know. It's fairly light so far." He opened a cupboard and pulled out two wineglasses. He held one toward Monica and raised his eyebrows.

"Yes, thank you," Monica said, opening the lid on the slow cooker and adding the potatoes. "I could do with a glass after the day I've had."

"Oh?"

She told Greg about Detective Stevens's call and the pathologist's determination that Marta had died by smothering, helped along by a possible overdose of beta blockers.

Greg poured them each a glass of red wine and held one out to Monica. She was raising the glass to her lips when she gasped.

Greg frowned. "What is it? Is something wrong?"

Monica shook her head. "Not wrong, no. But I just remembered something."

"Oh?" Greg raised his eyebrows.

"The pathologist thinks Marta had been smothered."

"And?" Greg smiled.

"When Dana and I went to Marta's house the day we found her body, I noticed a bed pillow was on the floor. I didn't think anything of it at the time. I can't remember now but either Dana or I picked it up and put it back on the bed." She looked at Greg. "But

"Honestly." Dorothy pursed her lips as the person continued to rattle the doorknob. "What is wrong with some people? The door is open," she called out.

A man stumbled into the room. As he got closer, a very unpleasant odor washed over Monica. He smelled like Flynn's, the dive bar next door—whiskey, spilled beer and stale cigarette smoke. His shirt and pants were worn and rumpled and his hair, so greasy he couldn't possibly have washed it recently, curled over his collar.

Dorothy made a face. "Oh, no, here's Don again. We haven't seen him since Marta passed away."

"Hi, sweetheart," Don said as he wove his way toward the counter.

Dorothy didn't say anything. She merely tightened her lips and gripped the edge of the counter.

"Can I help you?" she said when Don reached her.

"Gotta get me some food." He smiled, showing brownish teeth. "I'm a pretty good cook, did I tell you that?"

Dorothy withdrew into herself like a turtle withdrawing into its shell.

"Our volunteers are organizing the shelves," she said, her lips still clenched together. "I'm afraid you'll have to wait a few minutes."

Don turned to Monica and smiled. "Who's this? I don't think I've seen you around here before, sweetheart."

Monica gave a weak smile and turned to Dorothy for support.

Don's smile faded and he moved on, lurching toward the chairs in the waiting room.

"Who is that?" Monica said, watching as Don banged his knee against a table before collapsing into a chair.

"He's the thorn in our side," Dorothy said. "Everyone says he's harmless but I'm not so sure. He comes around regularly, usually after spending some time at Flynn's next door." She rolled her eyes. "He was particularly drawn to Marta Kuiper, who used to volunteer here." Dorothy fiddled with a pen on the counter. "Poor Marta! She was terribly quiet, a lovely lady but not very worldly, if you know what I mean." Dorothy raised an eyebrow at Monica.

Monica nodded.

"So she really didn't know how to deal with his attentions." Dorothy gave a half smile. "I would have told him to scram, quite frankly."

Monica was surprised. Dorothy appeared meek and mild on the surface but obviously she was made of sterner stuff.

"He used to follow Marta around while she stocked the shelves. Patrons aren't really allowed back there unless they're picking out their food, and then we only let them go in one at a time, but somehow he always managed to slip in unnoticed." She wrinkled her nose.

"Was he hostile toward Marta?" Monica said. "Do you think he meant to do her harm?"

"Oh, no. Not at all. For some reason he'd taken a shine to her. Maybe she reminded him of his mother, I don't know. You never know with people, do you?"

"I guess not."

"Is he homeless?"

"No. He said he has a room somewhere with a kitchenette. And he has a car, too. The muffler is gone and you can hear him coming from a mile away. When he's sober enough, he does odd jobs around town."

Don was now sitting quietly in the waiting room, rocking back and forth and singing softly to himself.

Monica looked at him. He seemed harmless enough, more a danger to himself than anyone else. Had he merely annoyed Marta or had she sensed something else in him—violent tendencies perhaps?

As Dorothy said, you never knew with people. Maybe Don had snapped, infuriated by Marta's lack of interest in him. Maybe he'd found out where she lived or had followed her home.

Somehow Monica couldn't see how he would have managed to give Marta an overdose of beta blockers, but perhaps she had accidentally done that herself? And he had found her nearly unconscious and had taken the opportunity to smother her?

Chapter 9

"Some man was pestering Marta?" Dana asked, her tone incredulous. "She never said."

Dana had stopped by Monica's cottage to let her know that Marta's funeral had been rescheduled now that the police had released the body.

Monica had been hoping to finish her lunch and get back to the kitchen to bake some cookies and to have another go at a cranberry coffee cake she was trying to perfect, but she could hardly turn Dana away.

Dana was sitting opposite her at the kitchen table with the cup of tea Monica had made her. She'd tossed her coat over the back of a chair but still had her silk and cashmere scarf wrapped around her neck. Her lipstick had left a smudge of pink on the edge of her teacup.

Monica explained about Don from the food pantry and how Dorothy had said he'd been fixated on Marta.

"That really is curious," Dana said. "Do you think he did it? Killed Marta, I mean."

"Dorothy, one of the volunteers at the food pantry, seems to know him and thinks he's harmless albeit annoying."

Monica finished the last of her sandwich and brushed some crumbs from her sweatshirt.

"Do you know someone named Cheryl DeSantis?" Monica asked. "I met her at the food pantry, too. She said she's your cousin."

Dana made a face. "She's our father's stepsister's daughter. When his mother died, his father remarried. Cheryl's mother was unfortunately part of the package. She had Cheryl at seventeen. Cheryl has always been a handful almost from the minute she was born," Dana hastened to explain. "Always in trouble of some sort whether it was shoplifting some eye shadow, drinking underage or driving without a license. You never knew what she was going to get up to next." She sighed.

"Cheryl said she used to live with Marta but she decided to leave because she wanted to get her own place."

Dana gave a surprisingly unladylike hoot of laughter. "She said that?" She shook her head. "Trust Cheryl to lie about something like that."

"So . . . that isn't true?" Monica pushed back her chair, picked up her plate and carried it to the sink.

"Not in the least. It couldn't be further from the truth." Dana pushed her teacup away, put her arms on the table and leaned toward Monica, who had taken her seat again. "Marta threw Cheryl out, pure and simple." She paused for a moment. "Actually, to put it more accurately, John and I threw Cheryl out. Marta didn't have the heart to do it."

She took a deep breath. "Cheryl abused Marta's kindness— coming home drunk at all hours, smoking in the house when Marta asked her not to." She blew out some air. "More than once Marta woke up, only to run into a strange man on her way to the bathroom!" She shuddered and turned to Monica. "Can you imagine? Cheryl brought men home with no regard for Marta's feelings or privacy."

Dana narrowed her eyes. "I wonder if the police will ever solve my poor sister's murder?" She stood up, put on her coat and gathered together her belongings. "Thank you for the tea," she said as Monica opened the door for her. Her expression turned serious and she put a hand on Monica's arm. "I do appreciate your support."

Monica watched as Dana backed down the driveway and then disappeared down the road.

Thoughts were spinning in her head. Cheryl had lied to her, which probably wouldn't have meant anything under ordinary circumstances. Cheryl sounded like the type of person who wouldn't think twice about stretching the truth if it suited her. But if Cheryl was the killer, she might have lied for a different reason. She might have realized that the truth would have given her a motive. Because no doubt she would have been extremely angry about being ejected from the comfort of Marta's house, only to end up living out of her car.

On the other hand, had Dana had an ulterior motive in telling Monica all this since it pointed a finger at Cheryl and away from herself?

• • •

Monica was reaching for her parka when Jeff knocked on the back door. She stifled a sigh as she opened it.

Jeff stamped his feet a couple of times, kicking off the snow, and walked into the kitchen.

Monica thought his expression was rather hangdog.

"What's up?" she said.

"Can I talk to you for a minute?"

"Sure." Monica glanced at the clock. Hopefully Kit would start on the cookies after he finished his lunch. He was definitely a self-starter, so Monica imagined she was worrying for no reason.

Jeff slouched in his chair, his elbows on the table and his chin in his hands. Monica got the impression he was nervous. What was it he wanted to tell her?

"Would you like a cup of coffee or tea?"

"Coffee would be great." Jeff's tone was glum.

Monica measured out the coffee, filled the carafe with water and poured it into the machine, all the while trying to imagine what Jeff had to tell her that had him looking the way he did.

She waited until the machine had finished, poured each of them a cup and carried them to the table.

"So," she said in what she hoped was a positive-sounding voice, "what is it you want to tell me?" She smiled reassuringly at Jeff.

Jeff reached for the sugar bowl and carefully added two spoonsful to his cup. He took his time stirring it in, all the while avoiding meeting Monica's eyes. Finally, he looked up.

"I don't know how to tell you this."

Monica felt her stomach clench. Was something wrong with Jeff? With Lauren? Had they broken up?

"Sometimes you just have to say it," she said, reaching out and patting Jeff's hand. "Whatever it is, we'll deal with it."

"I'm afraid you'll be disappointed in me, Sis."

Monica recalled her conversation with Greg. "I could never be disappointed in you." She smiled reassuringly. "So, come on. Out with it. It can't be that bad."

Jeff took a deep breath like someone about to dive into a pool.

"I'm thinking of selling the farm," he said in a rush.

Everything stood still. Monica felt her head swim. The ticking of the clock sounded exceptionally loud to her ears and she felt her breath speed up.

"But wh-why?" She could only stutter. "Why would you do that?"

Jeff spread his hand out, palm up, on the table. His other hand lay limply in his lap. He picked up his damaged arm with his good one. "Because of this."

He let his arm drop back into his lap.

"But aren't you managing? I thought you were managing okay. I mean, I know it hasn't been easy but . . ."

"Ever since I heard about that new therapy for injuries like mine, I haven't been able to stop thinking about it. I dream about it— about putting both my arms around Lauren's waist and not just one. About being able to cut my own meat and not need help buttoning my shirt." He choked back a sob.

"I didn't realize," Monica said. "I thought you had come to terms with it."

"I had. I have," Jeff said. "But I'm tired of it. I'm tired of simply managing. I want to be my old self again." He gave a mirthless laugh. "Of course, no one comes back from that hellish place like their old selves. There will always be scars."

He looked at Monica and straightened his shoulders. "So I want to sell the farm to get the money for the procedure."

"But what will you do? Where will you go without the farm?"

"I'll figure something out."

"Maybe the buyer would let you stay on and manage the farm."

Jeff immediately shook his head. "No, I'm afraid not." He ducked his head. "The buyer doesn't want the farm, he wants the land."

"The land? What is he going to do with it?"

"He's a developer. I suppose he'll build homes here."

"Not another one of those developments with huge modern houses? That will ruin Cranberry Cove."

Jeff shrugged. "Believe me. If there was another way . . . But I don't see how I could raise the cash otherwise."

Monica was stunned. She couldn't imagine bulldozers ripping the farm apart and houses being built where the bogs were now. What about all the birds and other small creatures that would be displaced?

"I wish I knew what to say to change your mind," she said.

She only wanted what was best for Jeff, she always had. And she could understand how much he wanted to be rid of his disability.

"But you don't even know if the procedure will work."

"I suppose it's a chance I'll have to take."

"How does Lauren feel about it?"

Monica wondered if Lauren was in favor of selling the farm. She'd spent a semester as an intern at a marketing firm in Chicago and had claimed she didn't mind returning to Cranberry Cove, where she was working remotely. But maybe she missed the big city and maybe she viewed the farm as an albatross around Jeff's neck. Without it, they would be free to move to Chicago. Jeff had a degree, no doubt he'd find a job.

She supposed she and Greg could move into Greg's apartment. It was small but had everything they needed—kitchen, bathroom, living room and bedroom. She could find a job herself. Perhaps the Cranberry Cove Inn or the Pepper Pot could use another hand in the kitchen.

Of course, nothing had been decided. Jeff hadn't made up his mind yet. She did know one thing though: this certainly wasn't the time for her and Greg to be thinking about having a baby.

Chapter 10

Jeff left Monica's, his shoulders still slumped, and Monica hastily donned her parka, hat and gloves. She arrived at the farm kitchen feeling slightly shaken and out of sorts.

"I've started on the cookies," Kit said when Monica arrived. "Can you smell them?" He took an exaggerated deep breath. "Ahhhh . . ."

Monica grunted. Kit looked at her strangely but didn't say anything.

What would Kit do if Jeff sold the farm? Monica wondered. Did Jeff not realize he was upending so many people's lives? The thought immediately made her feel guilty. If Jeff had a chance to fix his disabled arm, he deserved to take it.

Monica scooped some flour into a bowl from the large canister on the counter. As she was reaching for a measuring cup, she banged her elbow against the bowl and knocked it off the counter. It landed with a clatter on the tile floor.

Monica stared at the mess. She couldn't help it. She felt tears prick the backs of her eyelids and one escaped and rolled down her cheek.

Kit was rolling out cookie dough but stopped when he saw Monica's face.

"Is everything okay? What's wrong?"

"Nothing," Monica mumbled.

Kit gave her a stern look and stood with one hand on his cocked hip.

"Darling, something is obviously wrong. You know you can spill to me anytime. My lips are sealed." He put a finger to his lips.

Monica managed a wan smile. "Thanks, but I'm not ready to talk about it yet."

"You know where I am," Kit said, picking up his rolling pin. "Auntie Kit will be all ears whenever you need me."

Monica couldn't help but smile. Kit had a way of cheering her up no matter what. She managed to finish the batch of cookies but she didn't have the heart to do anything else. She wondered if she should call Greg. Talking to him always made her feel better. He was so practical and so calm.

She yanked off her apron and dusted off her sweatshirt. She would go to see him instead. Perhaps a hug would make her feel better.

"Kit, do you mind taking those cookies out of the oven when they're done? And if you could take them down to the farm store, I'd be grateful."

"Anything for you, sweetheart." Kit blew her a kiss. "You go take care of yourself."

Monica yanked her parka from the hook, nearly tearing it, and dashed out the door. All of a sudden she couldn't wait to see Greg — to have him put his arms around her and tell her everything was going to be okay.

She all but ran back to her cottage and jumped into her car. She was on the way into town when she happened to glance at her speedometer and was horrified to see she was driving twenty miles an hour over the speed limit. She immediately took her foot off the gas and slowed down.

She drove down Beach Hollow Road twice before finding a parking place when a pickup truck pulled out of a space in front of the diner.

The scent of bacon frying drifted from the diner as usual, and normally that would have made Monica's mouth water, but today it made her feel slightly sick to her stomach. She hurried past toward Book 'Em next door.

She burst into the shop without thinking but stopped short when several heads turned in her direction, questioning looks on their faces.

Greg's book club was gathered in a circle, having pulled together the old and sagging furniture Greg had collected for the shop. Phyllis Bouma, Cranberry Cove's head librarian, was there along with both Hennie and Gerda VanVelsen. There were a few other people who looked vaguely familiar to Monica but who she didn't actually know.

Greg looked up and smiled at Monica. The look on her face must have alarmed him because he jumped up and hastened toward her.

"Is something wrong?" He took her hands in his.

Monica hesitated. "I don't want to interrupt your book group."

"Let's go in my office." He turned to the assembled group. "I'll only be a minute if you'll please excuse me."

A murmur went through the group but no one objected.

"What is it?" Greg said as soon as he'd closed the door in back of them.

Monica told him about Jeff and how he was thinking about selling the farm.

"Whatever happens, we'll deal with it one way or another." Greg's voice was soothing. "I think it would be a shame to sell the farm—he's worked so hard to get it off the ground—but it's his decision and I can understand how he would want to take any chance possible to rid himself of his disability."

He put his arm around Monica's shoulders and squeezed.

"So please don't worry, okay?"

Monica nodded. She felt better already. Between them, she knew she and Greg could handle whatever came next.

As they were leaving, Monica saw Phyllis lean toward Hennie.

"I bet she came to tell him that there will soon be the pitter-patter of little feet in the house," she whispered loud enough for Monica to hear.

Both women turned and watched as Monica left the shop.

• • •

Monica felt her face burning. The women thought she was pregnant! They would find out soon enough that wasn't the case, she thought as she headed down the street toward Gina's shop.

Making Scents was empty when Monica got there.

"Hello?" she called out.

She heard rustling in the back room and Gina emerged with a box in her hands. She was panting slightly and there were Styrofoam peanuts clinging to her zebra-print leggings.

"I'm unpacking a shipment of essential oil candles that came in this morning." She blew out a puff of air and her bangs fluttered against her forehead. "I haven't carried them before, but I'm told they're the latest thing."

She put the box on the counter and reached for a utility knife.

"Be careful with that," Monica said in alarm.

Gina slit the tape on the carton. The knife slipped and nicked her finger.

"Ouch." She grabbed a tissue from the box on the counter and dabbed at the drop of blood that had formed on the tip of her finger.

Finally she got the box open. The fragrance of lavender, lemongrass and patchouli drifted out.

Monica's anxiety made her feel as if she was going to explode. She began to fiddle with the bottles displayed on the counter, but her hands were shaking slightly and she knocked one over.

Gina leveled her gaze at Monica. "You seem very agitated. Lavender is wonderfully calming." Her hand hovered over the display of bottles. She chose one, opened it and held it under Monica's nose. "Take a deep breath."

Monica tried to breathe but her chest was tight. She brushed the bottle aside and blurted out, "Did you know about Jeff and the farm? About selling, I mean?"

Gina put down the candle she was holding and placed both hands on the counter.

"Yes. But—" She held up a hand when Monica began to protest. "Jeff is merely thinking about it. Nothing has been decided."

"Why didn't you tell me?" Monica demanded.

"Jeff asked me to let him tell you himself." She held up a hand again as Monica began to protest once more. "Nothing has been decided. He isn't close to making up his mind yet."

Monica's shoulders drooped. "I realize it's his farm, but it affects me, too. And Greg," she added.

A bit of guilt nibbled at her. What had she given up to move to Cranberry Cove? A failing café in Chicago that would have soon been shuttered anyway? And she never would have met Greg if she hadn't agreed to help Jeff.

"I'm sorry," Monica said. "Of course it's Jeff's decision." She looked off into the distance. "And I can understand how he'd want to do anything that would restore the function to his injured arm."

Gina sighed. "The procedure is very experimental." She leaned her elbows on the counter and a piece of hair from her loose updo brushed her face. "I told Jeffie I think he should wait. There'll soon be something new and improved that won't be so iffy—that will be a sure thing."

"He told me about selling this morning so obviously he hasn't changed his mind."

"Don't you worry, sweetheart. Jeffie is meeting with the developer tomorrow. The man has only seen the property on a map, and now he wants to see it up close and personal." Gina gave a wicked smile. "And I plan to be there to make sure Jeff doesn't make any rash decisions."

• • •

Monica left Gina's shop and headed to Bart's Butcher Shop for some ground beef. Bart was wrapping some lamb chops in brown paper for a customer, carefully tying the package with a length of string.

He dropped the meat into a white paper bag and handed it to the customer.

"Here you go, Mr. Van't Hoff. You enjoy those chops now and say hello to the missus for me. How is she, by the way?"

Mr. Van't Hoff, an elderly gentleman with a pronounced stoop, frowned.

"Not so well. She has that old-timer's disease. What do they call it?"

"Alzheimer's?" Bart said, his brow creasing in concern.

"That's it," Mr. Van't Hoff said, smoothing his mustache with his index finger. "Horrible thing. But we're coping. Marion still enjoys the hymns she sings at church and the service on Sundays. We have to be grateful for the small blessings."

"That's so true," Bart said, saluting as Mr. Van't Hoff turned to leave. He smiled at Monica. "What can I do for you, young lady?"

Monica nearly snorted. Young lady? Hardly. If she and Greg did decide to have a baby, and she was able to conceive, she'd be considered a geriatric mother. Which was ridiculous since she didn't feel old at all.

"How's Jeff doing?" Bart said as he weighed the ground beef Monica had asked for. "The farm is such a wonderful addition to the community."

Monica felt overcome with guilt. What was everyone going to think if Jeff sold the farm to a developer? Who knew what horrors the man was planning on building. And Jeff would be the one they'd blame. She and Greg would hardly be able to hold their heads up, assuming they stayed in Cranberry Cove. Greg had put a lot of work into Book 'Em and the store was doing well. Would they be forced to move?

• • •

You're probably worrying for nothing, Monica told herself as she turned into the drive leading to the farm and her cottage. Jeff might not sell after all, and if he did, hopefully the townspeople would understand why.

Greg's car was in the driveway when Monica pulled up to the cottage, and Greg was in the process of carrying a carton full of books into the house.

"How was the rest of your day?" He smiled at Monica as she held the door open for him.

"Uneventful."

"I suppose that's good," Greg said wryly. "You're not still worried about Jeff and the farm, are you?" Greg put the carton on the kitchen table. "I spotted an estate sale on my way home and couldn't help myself." He grinned. "I'm hoping there might be a gem in here somewhere."

Monica got a bottle of wine out of the pantry. "I could use a glass tonight." She laughed. "I'm sure Phyllis Bouma would be shocked to see me drinking."

"Oh?" Greg looked at her with raised eyebrows. "I've seen Phyllis down a glass or two herself."

"As I left Book 'Em this afternoon I heard her whisper to Hennie that she wondered if I had come to tell you that I'm in the family way — which I'm sure is how she would oh-so-delicately put it."

Greg's face lit up. "That would be good news, wouldn't it?"

Monica poured two glasses of wine and handed one to Greg.

"We need to talk about that," she said, taking a sip. "With the possibility that Jeff might sell the farm, I don't think this would be the right time to start a family."

"Why not?" Greg was rifling through one of the books. "I don't see what difference Jeff selling the farm would make."

Monica swept a hand around the kitchen. "We'd most likely have to give up the cottage. Where would we live?"

"We're planning on building a house anyway. We could live above Book 'Em until it was completed."

"I just want to feel settled if and when we decide to have a baby."

Monica was grateful when Greg let the subject drop.

He continued to rummage through the carton of books. He pulled out another volume and flipped through it. Something fell out and landed on the floor.

"What's that?" Monica said.

Greg picked the item up and turned it over. "It's an old photograph." He handed it to Monica.

Three girls, their arms around each other, were in the picture. They were wearing plaid miniskirts and crew neck sweaters in soft pastels. Two of the girls looked to be around sixteen years old, while the girl in the middle looked slightly older. They were standing in front of an ornate cuckoo clock.

Monica gasped. "That's the clock that's in Marta Kuiper's living room."

Greg peered over Monica's shoulder. "Quite the monstrosity, isn't it? It could be a coincidence. Perhaps someone else had one just like it?"

"No. Dana told me it was one of a kind. Her father made it—he was a woodworker." Monica tapped the photograph. "I'm going to ask Dana about this."

"Why? Do you think it's significant?"

"I don't know. It could be, although probably not. Still, I think we should return the photograph to the owner, don't you think?"

Chapter 11

Monica was finishing up her first batch of cranberry scones for the day when she heard a vehicle rumbling down the path outside. She glanced out the window in time to see a bright red late-model pickup truck go by. Surprisingly, there wasn't a speck of dirt or slush on it. Monica was surprised—Jeff's truck was always mud-spattered.

Was that the developer coming to look at the farm? she wondered. She looked out the window again in time to see Gina's Mercedes go by. It was no longer the latest model—she was nursing it along, constantly fearful it would die on her and she'd be forced to buy a secondhand Kia.

The pickup pulled over a short way from the farm kitchen. As Monica watched, Jeff came out of the processing facility and walked over to greet the driver. *It must be the developer,* Monica decided. Gina had said he was coming today.

She whipped off her apron, wiped her hands on a paper towel and grabbed her jacket. She wanted to hear what the developer had to say.

Gina had parked in back of the pickup and was getting out of the car. Although she had toned herself down slightly—very slightly—since living in Cranberry Cove, she was obviously back and in fine form. She had on a miniskirt—Gina prided herself on having good legs—and sky-high peep-toe pumps. Her coat hung open and her skintight, low-cut mohair sweater was visible. She'd gone full tilt with her makeup as well: false eyelashes, sparkly shadow, crimson lipstick, and with her hair teased and sprayed into a blond haystack.

Monica could have sworn the developer's jaw dropped when he saw her walking toward him.

"Jeff," Monica yelled as she hurried to catch up with them.

Jeff didn't look thrilled to see Monica. If anything, he looked guilty.

"Monica, Gina, this is Bob Tapper. He's with Shoreline Development."

Tapper shook their hands with a firm grip. Gina batted her eyelashes at him.

They began walking. Gina's shoes were completely unsuitable to both the weather and the terrain. They hadn't gone more than a few yards when she stepped on an uneven patch of ground and rolled her ankle.

"Be careful there," Tapper said, grabbing Gina's elbow.

She took advantage of the situation to tuck her arm through his. Monica fell back behind them and watched in amazement as Gina swiveled her hips back and forth as she walked. Tapper was very solicitous, putting an arm around her to steady her and help her across an icy patch.

Monica dropped even farther behind. There was nothing to be gained by tagging along—she'd get all the details of the offer soon enough. She'd go back to the kitchen and get some baking done.

• • •

Monica was taking several cranberry coffee cakes out of the oven when the door burst open so suddenly it hit the wall opposite and ricocheted off, scaring Monica to the point where she nearly dropped the baking pan she was holding.

"What the . . ." Kit said.

Gina marched toward Monica. She was shivering and her shoes were covered in mud.

"The things we do for our children," she said, standing in front of the oven and holding her hands out toward the warmth. "I'm positively frozen and my ankle is sore."

Monica was about to point out that Gina had chosen what was possibly the least suitable outfit and shoes for the weather but then decided against it.

"What did you find out?"

Gina made a face. "Not much, I'm afraid. Jeffie brushed me off when it was time for them to talk business." Her expression brightened. "But I do have a dinner date with Bob Tapper tonight."

"Seriously?" Monica knew Gina knew her way around men, but she didn't realize she was that good.

"Yes. And he doesn't know it yet, but I'm going to pump him

for information." She gave a coy smile. "Somehow I don't think it will prove to be too challenging." Her expression was impossibly smug.

• • •

Monica decided to take a break midmorning. Her back was beginning to ache and so were her feet. How long could she continue to do this, she wondered — until she was fifty? Or sixty? Then she remembered Jeff might sell the farm, and she realized that that would create an entirely different set of worries.

The boxes were loaded with baked goods and Kit had promised to take them down to the store. She wouldn't be needed for an hour or two .

She thought she would pay Dana a visit and show her that photograph Greg had found in the old book. It might not mean anything, but her curiosity was getting the better of her.

Dana's car was in the driveway when Monica arrived. She pulled up in back of it. It was only when she got out of her car that she realized Dana was seated in the BMW, attempting to start the engine.

She must have noticed Monica because she opened the door and got out.

"I'm sorry. I didn't realize you were going somewhere. I can come back," Monica said.

Dana made a face. "No need. I can't seem to get my car started anyway, and I'm half frozen. Let's go inside and make some tea instead."

Monica followed Dana into the house. They had just taken off their coats when the cuckoo clock in the living room began signaling the hour. She had to admit, it had a certain unique charm.

Monica sat at the kitchen table while Dana fixed the tea. The kettle whistled, Dana poured hot water into two mugs, added tea bags and carried them to the table.

"I'd suggest we sit in the living room, but I think the kitchen is the least dreary room in this wretched house. At least it's a bit warmer. This old place is nothing but drafts." She reached for the milk and added a dribble to her cup. "And now that the police are considering Marta's death a possible homicide, they've asked me to stay here a bit longer." She sighed. "I've been giving serious thought to checking into the Cranberry Cove Inn. I can't seem to get warm in this place."

"I wanted to show you something." Monica reached for her purse and pulled out the photograph. She pushed it across the table toward Dana.

"As you know, my husband runs Book 'Em, the bookstore in town. He found this photograph in a book he got from an estate sale." Monica pointed at the picture. "If I'm not mistaken, that's your cuckoo clock in the photo."

Dana pulled a pair of reading glasses from her pocket and slipped them on.

"So it is. There isn't another one like it." She gave a wry smile.

"I thought you might know the girls in the photo?"

"Yes, certainly." Dana pointed to the girl with the blond braids wrapped around her head. "That's Marta." She frowned and held the photograph closer. "I don't know who that is," she said, indicating the girl in the middle, "but that" — she tapped the third figure — "is Marta's friend Joyce Murphy." She put the photo down on the table. "I think you met her. I heard they were inseparable at one time. I was quite young then so I really don't remember." She took off her glasses and rubbed her eyes. "I do know they were very close friends up until Marta's death. Joyce did a lot for Marta."

Dana ran her finger along a scratch in the tabletop. "Marta never learned to drive, she said it made her too nervous. Joyce took her everywhere. We're all grateful for Joyce's help." She picked up the photograph again. "Where did you say you found this?"

"It was tucked into a book Greg picked up at an estate sale."

"You can keep it." Dana pushed the photograph toward Monica. "I have no need for it."

Monica slipped the photograph back into her purse. She had no idea what she was going to do with it, but she had a feeling it might become important.

• • •

Monica was eating lunch when Gina burst through the door of the cottage. She was wearing the outfit she'd had on earlier, although she'd exchanged the sky-high pumps for a pair of suede stiletto-heeled over-the-knee boots.

"You won't believe it," she said as she rushed into Monica's kitchen.

Monica paused with her spoon in the air. "What won't I believe?"

Gina continued to flutter around the kitchen like a moth around a flame.

"Why don't you sit down?" Monica pulled out a chair to encourage her.

Gina heaved herself into the chair. "I saw that man again."

"Which man?" With Gina it was always a man, Monica thought.

"The one with the Jaguar and the silver hair."

"Oh." That had to have been John Kuiper.

"I was driving down Beach Hollow Road on my way back to the shop when I saw him. He was right in front of me. He'd just pulled out of a parking space in front of the diner."

Monica couldn't imagine where this was going.

"So I followed him."

"You what?" Monica's voice rose an octave.

Gina shrugged. "I figured why not? Jasmine is perfectly capable of handling the store while I'm gone. Besides, business isn't all that brisk this time of year. So I decided to take the time and follow him."

"Where did he go?"

"Home."

That answer struck Monica as somewhat anticlimactic. She struggled not to laugh.

Gina's eyes lit up. "He lives in a huge house in a tony section of Grand Rapids. You should see the place." She waved her hands in the air. "It must have five bedrooms at least, and I thought I saw a swimming pool and a cabana in the backyard."

"That's . . . interesting," Monica said, spooning up her soup. "But I don't see how —"

"I haven't told you the best part." Gina fiddled with the gold chain around her neck.

"What's that?" Monica patted her lips with her napkin.

"There was a *For Sale* sign on their front lawn."

"Are you looking for a house?"

Gina scowled. "No, silly." She held up a hand. "But wait. That isn't the best part."

Monica made what she hoped was an expectant-looking face.

"His wife—at least I'm pretty sure that's who it was—was leaving the house with a bunch of suitcases. The car was already loaded with things." Gina paused. "And she drove away alone!"

"So—"

"Don't you see? They're selling the house. The wife takes off with her car packed to the gills. No husband in sight."

Monica still didn't see what Gina was getting at.

"Come on," Gina exhorted. "It's obvious. They're getting a divorce," she announced with a flourish, throwing her hands into the air.

Only Gina could put all that together and come up with that conclusion, Monica thought.

"Maybe they're simply moving. You said there was a *For Sale* sign—"

"No. I'm positive they're splitting up. And guess who's going to be there to help him pick up the pieces?" She batted her eyelashes at Monica and grinned. "All I have to do is find a way to run into him and introduce myself."

• • •

Monica kept thinking about what Gina had told her as she creamed butter and sugar, sifted flour and rolled out dough. If Gina was right and John was divorcing his wife, he would most likely end up losing money in any settlement. Or maybe his wife's expensive tastes combined with his own had already sent him into bankruptcy. If that was the case, he might be hard up for cash, which meant that he would have had a much bigger stake in whether or not Marta agreed to sell their property to that developer who had made the offer. Which, in turn, would give him a motive for murder after all.

Monica really wanted to know one way or the other. She

thought about it all afternoon and at four o'clock whipped off her apron and told Kit she had an appointment.

"Be sure to finish the compote," she said as she grabbed her coat. "I'm delivering it tomorrow morning."

Kit gave a playful salute. "Aye, aye, Captain."

Monica started to shut the door but then opened it again.

"I really do appreciate it," she said. "Thank you."

• • •

It was a bit of a drive to Grand Rapids from Cranberry Cove and Monica was glad that the roads had been cleared of the recent snow. Most of the traffic was headed in the opposite direction so she made good time. She enjoyed the ride—she had the radio on a station playing soothing music and it gave her time to think.

She was beginning to believe that John was the most likely suspect in Marta's murder. He was a doctor and would know what effect an overdose of Marta's beta blocker pills would have had on her.

But she wasn't going to jump to any conclusions just yet.

John and his wife lived in a high-end neighborhood where the houses were set back among mature trees and all the homes on the street were large and expensive.

Monica found the street Gina had mentioned and drove down it slowly. Most of the homes were fairly modern with circular drives and impressive entryways. Large pine trees dotted the properties and one or two still had their Christmas lights attached. The houses were set fairly far apart and it didn't take her too much time to find the Kuiper residence.

Like its neighbors, the house was enormous. And just as Gina had said, a large *For Sale* sign with the realtor's name on it was plunked in the middle of the lawn.

Monica pulled up to the curb and killed the engine. She turned up her collar, pulled on her gloves and got out of the car. She walked partway down the driveway, and from that vantage point the house looked even larger.

She was about to turn around lest someone come out of the house to ask what she wanted, when the front door opened.

Monica froze. What excuse could she give for standing in the middle of their driveway?

But neither John nor his wife came out the open door. Instead, it was an older couple carrying what looked to be an antique Tiffany lamp. Or rather, the man was struggling with it while the woman marched ahead of him, unencumbered by anything save the patent leather pocketbook she was clutching to her rather ample bosom.

Monica was about to turn around and head to her car when the woman smiled and walked up to her.

"Great sale." She jerked her head in the direction of the Kuipers' house. "A lot of good stuff still left. I tried to get Tom here to spring for the set of silver—Grand Baroque by Wallace, which has always been a favorite of mine—but the man's too stingy for his own good." She threw the last over her shoulder at her husband, who was patiently waiting. "Good luck," she said to Monica as she started to walk away. "I hope you find something you like."

Monica was headed toward her car when a woman came down the street and turned into the driveway. She was wearing yoga pants and an expensive white North Face parka.

She nodded at Monica as she passed.

"Hello." Monica rushed after her. "Are you a neighbor of the Kuipers?"

The woman stopped and looked Monica up and down. She brushed away a strand of hair that had blown onto her forehead and Monica noticed the diamond tennis bracelet that slid up and down her arm.

"Yes, we're neighbors." She pointed to the house next door. "I live over there."

"I'm sort of surprised that their house is for sale," Monica said. "I haven't seen them in a while." She crossed her fingers behind her back.

"Then you must not know." The woman leaned closer to Monica, enveloping her in a cloud of Joy perfume. "They're having financial troubles and had to put the house on the market."

"Oh." Monica feigned shock. "I had no idea. Like I said, it's been a while . . ."

"Then there was that other business. I'm sure you've read about it."

"I didn't—"

"Anyway, I'm checking out their sale," the woman said, cutting Monica off. "They had a Jenny Saville painting I've always liked. It was over the mantelpiece. I hope they're selling it." She waved to Monica as she strode away.

Monica walked back to her car. Her trip had certainly been worthwhile, she thought as she put the car in gear and drove away.

She wondered what that "other business" was that the woman had referred to. She planned to do a computer search on John Kuiper as soon as she got home.

• • •

Monica couldn't wait to get home and to her computer. There was an accident on the highway, not much more than a fender bender, but it held her up for an extra half an hour.

It was dark by the time she pulled into her driveway. No lights were on in the cottage. Greg must still be at the shop.

Mittens was waiting for Monica when she switched on the light. Monica picked her up and scratched her under her chin. Mittens closed her eyes and purred loudly but soon became bored and jumped down.

Monica hung up her coat and set up her laptop on the kitchen table. She turned it on but then thought of something and jumped up to look in the refrigerator. In her excitement she had forgotten all about dinner. She had eggs and bacon—they could have breakfast for dinner, she decided.

Her laptop sprang to life, showing a picture of Mittens curled up in her favorite armchair. Monica brought up a search engine and typed in John Kuiper's name.

There were numerous references to him on doctor rating sites. One had an old picture taken when his hair was still dark and only threaded with gray. Monica had to admit, he was a good-looking man.

She continued to scroll past the entries for papers he had written or cowritten until she came to an article in the *Grand Rapids*

Press. She pushed her chair back and stared at the screen. This must be what that woman had been referring to.

The headline was big and bold: *Surgeon Sued for Malpractice After Patient Dies.*

Greg came home while Monica was reading. She looked up when the back door opened.

"You won't believe what I've discovered," she said.

Greg's look was one of bemusement. "What have you discovered?" he said, bending down and giving Monica a kiss on the cheek. "You seem excited, whatever it is."

Monica told him about John Kuiper's house being for sale and how he seemed to be selling off possessions.

"Gina was convinced that he and his wife are getting a divorce and that he needs money for the settlement," Monica said. "But then I found this."

She turned the computer around so Greg could read the article.

He whistled. "That settlement figure sure has a lot of zeroes, doesn't it?" He shrugged off his coat. "But that's what malpractice insurance is for. It probably won't cost him a penny."

"I don't know," Monica said. "What if he wasn't insured for that much? It's a huge sum. Maybe he thought he'd save money by taking out less insurance."

"That could be." Greg stroked his chin. "Of course, his premiums will go up after this. That alone could put someone in bankruptcy, I would imagine."

"I did notice that his wife has extremely expensive tastes as well."

Greg shook his head. "I think I'll stick with being a bookstore owner." He smiled. "A lot less stress."

"I do think it gives him a motive for murder though," Monica said.

Chapter 12

Monica and Greg were in the living room relaxing, each with their respective book. A fire crackled in the hearth and Monica had a throw pulled up over her legs. Wind was beating at the windows and she felt like burrowing under the afghan and not coming out until spring arrived.

She was about to get up to make some hot cocoa when there was a frantic knocking on the front door.

Greg looked at his watch. "It's ten o'clock. A little late for someone to drop by. Maybe it's Jeff?" He got up from his chair. "I have to admit to being a little gun-shy ever since Dana showed up on our doorstep claiming that someone was trying to kill her."

Monica felt a blast of cold air as Greg opened the front door. Seconds later, Gina burst into the room. She was wearing a short black cocktail dress with a plunging neckline, a fox fur jacket and ridiculously high heels with ribbons that wound up her legs like a ballerina's pointe shoes.

"Gina! Why don't you sit down," Greg said. "Can I take your coat?"

Gina pulled the jacket around her more closely. "No, I'm still half frozen. Will this winter never end? I wish I could afford to take a cruise to get away from it. But thank you anyway." She smiled at Greg.

"How was your dinner date with the developer? That was tonight, wasn't it?" Monica said, putting down her book. "Did you have a good time?"

Gina crossed her arms over her chest. "No," she said tersely. "I went to all this trouble" — she indicated her outfit and her makeup and hairdo — "and he took me to some dive on the highway just outside of town. It was one of those places with neon lights in the shape of a cocktail glass outside and ratty décor that was in style about thirty years ago." She shuddered. "The food was terrible — greasy and simply horrible." She shuddered again. "The cheap so-and-so. I thought he'd spring for the Cranberry Cove Inn at least. He must be rolling in dough."

"Maybe not," Greg said. "It can be a bumpy business."

"No kidding," Gina said.

"Can I get you something to drink?" Greg said, hesitating by the door to the kitchen.

"A martini?" Gina said. "I need something to calm my nerves."

Greg looked momentarily shocked but quickly assumed a more neutral expression.

"Shaken or stirred?" he asked, one eyebrow raised in inquiry and a smile playing around his lips.

"Frankly, I don't give a hoot. Lots of gin and only a whisper of vermouth," Gina called after him as he headed into the kitchen.

Gina let out a sigh, sounding not unlike a horse snorting its displeasure. She looked at Monica. "The dinner wasn't a total loss at least, even if I do get killer heartburn later from that dish they had the nerve to call steak au poivre."

"Oh?" Monica raised her eyebrows.

"I got him to talk about the farm and the development he's planning. Although I have to say it wasn't easy. He wanted to talk about *us*. He actually thought I was going to go back to his cheap motel room with him, which probably smells of stale cigarette smoke, all because he bought me a couple of drinks and a twenty-dollar dinner."

"But what did he say about the farm and the development?" Monica was feeling impatient and anxious at the same time.

"He said he plans to build a mall with all kinds of shops and an upscale chain restaurant." Gina snorted. "Not that he knows a thing about good restaurants."

Monica found herself clenching her fists and forced herself to relax.

"I can't imagine a mall in Cranberry Cove, can you? We're a sleepy little town, not a big city. Why would we need a mall?" Monica simply couldn't picture it. "And what about all the merchants along Beach Hollow Road? It will put them out of business. Mall stores can offer a larger selection and often at a better price."

Monica jumped out of her seat. "We have to convince Jeff not to sell! It would ruin Cranberry Cove."

"As much as I'd love to have a mall so close at hand — you know how I love to shop — I have to agree with you. Unfortunately, it's not just a matter of Jeff refusing to sell the farm."

Monica stopped pacing. "Oh?"

"The developer has his eye on another piece of property as well. It's a matter of convincing all the siblings to sell, he told me. When they couldn't give him an answer right away, he went looking for another spot to develop. That's how he came to be interested in Sassamanash Farm."

That must be the Kuiper land, Monica thought.

"So it's a choice between Jeff's farm and this other property?"

"I'm afraid so. Even if Jeff won't sell, those other people probably will, and there will be nothing to stop the wretched Bob Tapper from building his mall."

• • •

Sunday morning it was overcast and rather dreary. Greg lit a fire in the fireplace while Monica made cranberry pancakes and fried bacon for their breakfast. They finished their meal and adjourned to the living room, which was cozy and warm from the now glowing logs in the fireplace.

Greg had brought in the Sunday papers and within minutes the sections were spread all over the carpet. He was relaxing in his favorite chair and Monica was curled up on the sofa, Mittens at her feet and a throw pulled up over her legs.

She flipped through the Lifestyle section of the paper but stopped when she came to a Macy's ad for baby clothes—darling onesies, cozy pajamas and colorful play clothes.

She suddenly felt a strong pang that nearly took her breath away. Should she and Greg consider having a child? She could picture a darling little boy with Greg's thick thatch of dark hair. Or an adorable little girl with curls like hers.

But what if she set her heart on a baby and it didn't come to pass? Wouldn't that be even worse than putting the whole idea out of her mind once and for all?

"A penny for your thoughts," Greg said, smiling.

Monica quickly closed the section of the newspaper and tossed it on the coffee table.

"Daydreaming," she said. "Of warm blue waters and cloudless skies."

"Can I join you?" Greg said.

"Of course."

• • •

Monica overslept on Monday. It wasn't something she normally did, but she'd been so tired lately for some reason. She supposed it was the stress of everything that had happened. It wasn't every day that someone showed up on your doorstep claiming that somebody was trying to kill them.

She had to hurry. She glanced at the clock over the stove. She'd promised to deliver the cranberry compote to the Pepper Pot first thing in the morning.

"Need a hand with that?" Kit said, appearing from the storage room when Monica arrived at the farm kitchen. He yawned and swept a hand through his hair.

"You still haven't made up with Sean?" Monica said in disbelief.

"Not yet." Kit stiffened his shoulders. "I'm still quite mad at him. I'm waiting until I cool off a bit, otherwise, my dear, I have no idea what might come out of this mouth of mine."

Monica laughed. "I still hate to think of you sleeping in the storage room."

"Don't worry about me." Kit flapped a hand. "I'm fine."

Kit grabbed several jars of compote off the shelf and transferred them to the box Monica had open on the counter.

"But today is your day off," Monica said. "It's Monday."

Kit shrugged. "I don't have anything pressing to do. I'm happy to lend a hand."

Monica took a deep breath. She hated being rushed but there was nothing she could do about it.

The drive into town didn't take long. She drove down the narrow alley that led to the back of the Pepper Pot and the delivery entrance. She parked and wrestled the first carton out of the car.

The back door was propped open and the aroma of garlic and onions sautéing made her mouth water.

Mickey Welch, the affable new owner of the restaurant, met Monica halfway. He was wearing a plaid flannel shirt with the sleeves rolled up, showing his powerful forearms. He had a youthful face but his age was apparent in his thatch of silver gray hair.

"Here, let me take that," he said when he saw Monica struggling with the box.

He easily hefted the carton under his arm and led Monica into the storeroom, where he placed it on a shelf.

"Are there more?"

"Yes, but there's no need —"

He gave a big smile, showing a gap between his front teeth. "My mama taught me better than to let a lady — and a pretty one at that — carry something when I'm empty-handed."

He was flirting with her! Monica was taken aback. It had been a long time since that had happened. She hoped she wasn't turning red.

Welch finished unloading the boxes and putting them on the shelf. He tapped one of them.

"Our new dessert with your cranberry compote has been a big hit. You'll have to come in and sample it sometime."

"I will," Monica said, suddenly anxious to leave. The way he was looking at her was making her feel as awkward as a teenager.

"Do you mind if I leave my car here while I run to the hardware store?" Monica said.

"Not at all. I'll keep an eye on it for you."

Since she was in town, she might as well run a few errands, Monica decided. She needed some picture hooks to hang the painting she and Greg had purchased on a trip to Traverse City and which they had not yet found a spot for. Finally they had agreed to hang it over the sofa.

Monica strolled down Beach Hollow Road toward the hardware store. The sun was out and she could feel its warmth on her face. It seemed to promise better days to come.

She was almost to the diner when someone coming in the opposite direction slammed into her hard. It felt intentional and Monica quickly glanced up to see who it was.

A rather scruffy-looking man, unshaven and smelling of alcohol, was wearing a jacket with the hood pulled up so that it shadowed his face. He shoved a piece of folded paper at Monica and continued on toward the other end of the street.

Monica was so stunned she stopped in the middle of the sidewalk. A woman in a red beret with a pompom on top gave her a reproachful look as she uttered *well* under her breath and walked around Monica.

Monica moved closer to the buildings and stood under the awning of Twilight as she unfolded the piece of paper.

The note was written in block letters and was short and sweet but no less chilling.

Tell Jeff not to sell the farm. Or else.

Or else what? Monica shivered. She quickly turned and looked down the street but the man had already disappeared from view. There was something familiar about him but Monica couldn't place him. Her hands began to shake and she dropped her purse. Her lipstick rolled out of the open top and she chased it across the sidewalk.

"Is something wrong?" Tempest Storm swept out of her shop in a swirl of burgundy velvet, the various amulets and chains around her neck clinking and clanking.

"I'm fine," Monica said, although she knew her voice was unsteady. "I haven't eaten," she fibbed, "and I think I got a bit shaky."

"Come on inside. I have some organic protein bars stashed in a drawer. You do look rather pale."

Monica shook her head. "I'll be okay. Don't worry."

All she could think about was running down to Book 'Em to talk to Greg.

Finally reassured, Tempest went back into the shop and Monica continued down the street toward the bookstore. She'd forgotten all about the hardware store in her panic over the note.

She stood outside Book 'Em for a minute or two to try to pull herself together. The words *or else* kept running through her head like a musical refrain.

She felt a bit calmer as she opened the door to Book 'Em. This might simply be someone's idea of a not-so-funny practical joke.

"What a lovely surprise," Greg said as he came out from behind the counter where he'd been filling out some papers. He took Monica's hands, pulled her close, and gave her a quick kiss.

Monica had waited until her breathing had slowed but it suddenly increased again.

Greg looked at her curiously. "Is something wrong?"

"I don't know." Monica fished in her pocket and pulled out the note. "Someone bumped into me on the sidewalk and handed me this."

Greg's eyebrows shot up and he took the piece of paper Monica was holding out. He opened it up and read the message.

"What the . . ." His hand tightened on the piece of paper. "We need to go to the police with this." He flicked a finger against the note. "No one should be allowed to try intimidation tactics like this and get away with it."

"What would the police be able to do?" Monica said. "There's no name and I have no idea who the guy was who handed it to me. Someone obviously slipped him a few dollars to do it."

Greg's arm dropped to his side. "You're right. But I think it would be good to let them know."

"I'll give Detective Stevens a call," Monica promised, although she really couldn't see any point to it.

But she did feel better as she left the shop. She smiled. Greg seemed to have that effect on her.

She still couldn't imagine someone writing a note like that. What was the purpose? Had someone in town learned about the offer for Jeff's farm and the possible development being planned?

As Monica walked toward the Pepper Pot, something else occurred to her. According to Gina, the developer was interested in two properties—Jeff's and the farmland belonging to the Kuipers. But he was only in the market for one of them, not both.

If John Kuiper was really in deep financial trouble, the sale of the family farm could save him from bankruptcy. But only if Jeff decided not to sell.

Monica could easily imagine someone like John writing that note and then paying someone to deliver it.

She shivered. She had no doubt that John could be a ruthless enemy and she had the terrible feeling that he was aiming his wrath at Jeff and Sassamanash Farm.

• • •

Kit was starting on a batch of cookies when Monica got back to the farm kitchen.

He gave Monica a slightly peculiar look. "Is everything okay, dear?" He frowned. "You look positively peaked."

"A bit tired is all," Monica said, quickly turning her back and reaching for her apron.

Kit didn't look convinced, but he went back to spooning dough studded with cranberries and chocolate chips onto a cookie sheet.

An hour later, Monica had filled several boxes with baked goods. She put them on the cart, said goodbye to Kit and trundled them down to the store.

The store was empty. Nora was leaning on the counter with her head propped in her hands. She looked up quickly when she heard Monica open the door.

She helped Monica arrange the cookies, scones and slices of cranberry apple cake in the case.

Nora was normally very quick, with swift and efficient movements, but today she seemed to be dragging. There were lines of weariness around her eyes that weren't usually there.

"Are you feeling okay?" Monica asked as she straightened a doily on one of the display trays.

"I suppose I should tell you, although it's early days yet, and we're really not telling anyone. You never know what might happen." Nora leaned against the counter and crossed her arms over her chest. "There's going to be a new little one in the family come August."

"That's wonderful!" Monica hesitated. "Isn't it?" she said, giving Nora a hug. She looked at Nora's face. "You're not happy about it."

"It's not that I'm unhappy," Nora said. "It's just not the best timing. I've got two little ones who already tire me out. I can't imagine coping with a baby as well. Just the thought of midnight feedings and all the laundry makes me want to burrow under the covers and sleep." She smiled. "But I am sure it will be a blessing when it arrives. It always is. Besides" — she straightened some jars of cranberry jelly on the counter — "is there ever really a perfect time to have a baby?"

Monica thought about that as she checked the shop's inventory of cranberry preserves and packages of dried cranberries. Nora was right — was there ever really a perfect time to have a baby? If everyone waited for the perfect moment, the human race would have died out a long time ago.

Monica was about to leave the store when the door opened and Dana walked in.

"Oh," Monica said, surprised to see her. Dana seemed slightly rattled—her face was paler than usual and her hair was slightly rumpled.

"Can we talk?" Dana said, taking Monica by the arm.

"Sure." Monica glanced at Nora. "But let's go back to my cottage."

"Let me take you to lunch. We could go to the Cranberry Cove Inn. Is it still as popular as it used to be?"

"I'm really not dressed—"

Dana waved a hand. "You look fine, but if you'd rather change and meet me there in an hour?"

Monica raced back to the cottage, slipped into her good black slacks, a merino wool sweater, and put a gold chain around her neck. She ducked into the bathroom and powdered her nose and freshened her lipstick.

She arrived at the Cranberry Cove Inn just as Dana was getting out of her car.

"I appreciate your joining me," Dana said as they walked toward the door of the restaurant.

The maître d' greeted them with a flourish and showed them to a table by the window. They had a view of the lake, where a layer of fog hovered just above the surface and the water was gray and chilly-looking.

The Inn had recently redecorated the dining room, and Monica assumed it was in response to competition from the Pepper Pot. Everything had been updated, from the curtains to the tablecloths, and was sleek and modern. It made a good contrast to the pub-like feel of the Pepper Pot but was still elegant enough for the special occasions like anniversaries and birthdays that Cranberry Cove residents generally splurged on there.

The waiter stopped at their table, filled their water glasses and handed them menus. He took their drink orders, a glass of Chardonnay for Monica and an old-fashioned for Dana.

"The special of the day is potato encrusted walleye with garlic mashed potatoes and roasted vegetables," he said when he'd finished writing down their drink order. "I'll give you a few minutes to decide. Take your time, ladies."

"Thank you for meeting with me," Dana said, turning her fork over and over. "I wanted to tell you that I've gotten some of my memory back."

"Oh?" Monica sat up a little straighter.

"Not everything, I'm afraid, but enough to scare me silly."

The waiter appeared with their drinks and placed them at their elbows.

"Ready to order, ladies?"

Dana tapped her menu. "I'll have the walleye." She handed the menu to the waiter.

"And you, miss?"

"I'll have the butternut squash soup and a house salad with vinaigrette, please."

"Very good."

"What have you remembered?" Monica said as the waiter walked away.

Dana took a sip of her drink. "I remember being at Marta's house now. That part is much clearer. She wasn't downstairs and she didn't answer when I called her, but I knew she had to be home since the front door was unlocked. I went up to her bedroom. It was early afternoon so I suppose she was taking a nap since she was lying in bed. Someone was bending over her with their back to me."

Monica could see Dana's chest rise and fall as she became more agitated and her hands shook as she raised her glass to her mouth. She took a gulp of her old-fashioned and coughed.

"I asked them what they were doing. Was something wrong with Marta?"

"Who was it? Could you see their face?"

Dana shook her head. "Not then. But they did turn around. I think they must have come after me. That's why I was driving the way I was, trying to escape." Dana shook her head. "But that's where my memory fades, I'm afraid. I can't seem to remember who it was or what they looked like."

"Could you tell if they were male or female?"

"Not even that, unfortunately." Dana looked down into her cocktail glass. She rubbed the skin on her forehead. "I've tried and tried but all I've managed to do is give myself a headache." She gave a small smile that disappeared so quickly Monica wondered if she had imagined it.

"I do remember being terribly frightened and running down the stairs and out to my car." She frowned. "That must have been why I was driving so fast and why I had the accident." Her forehead puckered. "The police thought I banged my head on the steering wheel but maybe that person, whoever it was, had hit me over the head?"

Dana downed the rest of her old-fashioned. Monica had barely touched her wine.

"I so wish I could go home." Dana's voice became plaintive. She fussed at the silk scarf around her neck. "But the police want me to stay." She gave a bitter laugh. "They haven't ordered me to stay, but they made it plain nonetheless." She pushed her empty glass to the side and leaned her elbows on the table. "I'm only an hour away in East Lansing but that didn't hold any sway with them."

The waiter appeared with their lunches and placed the plates in front of them with a flourish before bowing and disappearing.

"I wonder if I should move to the Inn here," Dana said, picking up her knife and fork. "I can't stand that house another minute. And if someone is out to get me, they'd have a harder time finding me here."

Monica reached for the salt. "Do you really think someone is after you? If you knew who the killer was, certainly you would have told the police by now. And surely the killer must realize that."

"I don't know." Dana sectioned off a piece of her fish. Her movements made it look as if she was dissecting it. "You have to be sure they haven't left any bones in," she explained. "Chefs can be so careless. I got one caught in my throat once when I was young and it frightened me. It was years before I was willing to eat fish again.

"That house is so cold and drafty and dreary, and it doesn't seem to make any difference how high I set the thermostat, I can never get warm. And every noise, no matter how innocent, makes me jump. I'm beginning to think it really would be more bearable if I moved here to the Inn." She laughed. "There's a view of the lake, but frankly, looking out at that cold gray water simply gives me the chills."

• • •

Monica decided to stop by Book 'Em after finishing her lunch with Dana. Several people were browsing the shelves, which were filled willy-nilly with used books, loosely divided into sections like Romance, Mystery and Fantasy. The Nonfiction section was a gigantic hodgepodge where you might find a book on ornithology sitting between a cookbook and a book on the history of medieval England. Greg always claimed he was going to straighten everything out as soon as he had time, but so far that hadn't happened.

An older woman was sitting in one of the sagging slipcovered armchairs with a stack of books on the table beside her. She was leafing through a volume and humming softly to herself.

Another patron, a young man with a beard, was sitting on the floor in the Mystery section, his back against one of the book-shelves.

Greg came out of his office and smiled when he saw Monica.

"I was about to make some coffee. Would you like some?"

"No, thanks," Monica said, unwinding her scarf. "I've already had a cup. I had lunch with Dana Bakker. She's moving to the Cranberry Cove Inn."

Monica followed Greg into his office, which was barely bigger than a closet. Piles of papers littered his desk and books were stacked next to it on the floor.

Greg sank into his office chair and Monica took the chair opposite. The space was so tight that their knees were almost touching.

"Dana told me that she's recovered some of her memory." Monica relayed her conversation with Dana to Greg. "Now that she's remembered a bit more of what happened, she's more frightened than ever."

"I don't blame her," Greg said, pushing some books out of the way with his foot. "Hopefully the police will soon discover what really happened."

"I can't help but wonder if Dana isn't spinning us a grand tale — amnesia, remembering only bits and pieces of what happened, a car accident because someone was trying to kill her."

"It does seem a bit far-fetched." Greg rocked back and forth in his chair. "Although she certainly seemed believable. And I rather like her. But at the same time, there is a lot of money at stake. If the brother needs money, maybe Dana does, too?"

"Hmmm," Monica said. "According to Dana, she barely knew her older sister. She was still quite young when Marta was already in her teens. Maybe there's more to Marta than we've been told?"

Greg cocked his head. "It's possible."

"You know that photograph you found in that book, where it turned out two of the girls pictured were Marta and her friend Joyce?"

"Yes."

"I wonder who the third girl was. Maybe she can tell us something more about Marta. I'm not convinced that Dana is telling us everything she knows."

"You're not?"

"No. It's a gut feeling. I think there's something she's leaving out."

Greg looked doubtful. "You're not usually one to have gut feelings," he said with a smile. "You usually rely on facts."

"I know. But I'm after facts — isn't that sort of the same thing?"

Greg didn't look convinced.

"Where did you get that book?" Monica said. "If the owner of the book kept that photograph, maybe they know something that might be helpful. They must have known Marta after all."

"I don't know. It was an estate sale, although I believe they were putting the house up for sale because the owner was moving to a nursing home. I suppose you could give it a try."

Monica pulled a pad and pen from her purse. "What was the address?"

She wrote down the directions Greg gave her, closed her notebook and slipped it back into her purse.

"I'll let you know what I find out," she said as she stood up.

Chapter 13

Monica found the house easily enough. It was one of the older homes in Cranberry Cove, a moderate-sized Dutch colonial about a mile from Sassamanash Farm.

A large sign on the front lawn read *Estate Sale 10:00 a.m. to 6:00 p.m.*, and underneath, in smaller letters, *Cranberry Cove Estate Sale Management.*

The front door opened as Monica was walking up the flagstone path and a woman emerged clutching an old-fashioned music box. She smiled at Monica as she passed.

Monica stepped inside. A set of polished wood stairs led from the foyer to the second floor. The living room was off to the right and it was obvious that several pieces had already been sold and removed. Indentations were visible in the carpet where chairs must have once stood and most of the tables and end tables were bare of knickknacks.

A woman bustled over to Monica immediately. She had a clipboard under her arm and was wearing a royal blue pantsuit with a flowered silk blouse. Her blue eye shadow, which had been liberally applied, matched her outfit.

"May I help you?" she said, cocking her head to one side. "Is there anything in particular you would like to see? There are some fine Baker pieces, or are you more interested in china and crystal? I'm afraid an awful lot has been sold already."

"Actually, I wanted to speak to the owner of the house. Or one of their relatives perhaps?"

The woman's glance darted around the room and her mouth puckered as if she had tasted something sour.

"The daughter is in the kitchen. But I don't know . . ." She looked around as if hoping to pluck an answer out of the air.

Monica put a reassuring hand on the woman's arm. "I won't disturb her. I promise. I just have a quick question for her."

"I suppose it's all right." The woman patted her lacquered hair nervously. "It's straight down the hall." She pointed toward the foyer.

Monica found the kitchen easily enough. Several cupboard

doors were open and boxes were lined up on the counter. A woman was bending over reaching into one of the lower cabinets.

She straightened when she heard Monica's footsteps. She gave a tired smile.

"I'm afraid nothing in here is for sale," she said.

She was short and slight and was wearing a pair of pants that looked too big on her, as if she had recently lost weight. Her light brown hair was liberally mixed with gray and was held back from her face with a tortoiseshell barrette.

"I wasn't looking to buy anything," Monica said.

The woman gave her a quizzical look.

"My husband—he owns the bookstore in town—bought some books here—"

"If he wants to return them, he'll have to talk to Louise. She's with the estate sales company. I don't have anything to do with it. I hired them to deal with it. It's been enough work getting my mother settled into the nursing home without taking this on as well."

"He doesn't want to return any of the books," Monica reassured her. "He found an old photograph tucked into one of the books and thought the owner might want it. They might have forgotten it was in there."

"I imagine that belonged to my mother." She placed the pot she was holding in one of the boxes on the counter. "I'm afraid we had to put her in a nursing home. She fell and broke her hip and it's obvious she can't manage on her own anymore. We tried to get her to move sooner, but she wouldn't hear of it." She gave a weary smile.

"Do you think she'd mind if I visited her and gave her the photograph?"

"Of course not." The woman smiled. "I imagine she would enjoy the company. We try to get there as often as we can but . . ." She shrugged. "The nursing home is in Holland. Not terribly far, but you know how it is." She bent and pulled another pot from the cupboard. "It's called Windhaven Terrace. My mother's name is Mildred Visser."

Monica glanced at her watch as she left the estate sale. She had just enough time to drive to Holland and talk to Mrs. Visser. She sat in her car and dialed Greg at the bookshop. She'd ask him to pick up something for dinner.

• • •

Windhaven Terrace was near the town center of Holland not far from the Hope College campus, where students bundled in winter gear with books tucked under their arms strolled to and from the Dutch revival buildings.

Monica found the nursing home and pulled into the parking lot. A woman was helping an elderly man into her car and another was pushing a frail-looking woman, huddled in a blanket, in a wheelchair.

Monica found the entrance, went up to the desk and asked for Mildred Visser. She hesitated when the receptionist asked her name but finally said she was an acquaintance of Mrs. Visser's daughter.

That seemed to satisfy the woman and she picked up the telephone on her desk and had a short conversation with someone on the other end.

"Third floor, number three-oh-seven," she said, handing Monica a visitor's badge.

The lobby was bright and clean, if a bit worn, but there were fresh flowers in a vase on a coffee table where various magazines were scattered. Monica found the elevator and headed up to the third floor.

The hallway was brightly lit and smelled of lemon air freshener. Monica found Mrs. Visser's room and knocked on the door.

"Come in," a rather frail voice answered.

The room was small with space for a hospital bed, a recliner, a small armchair and a desk. A flat-screen television was mounted on the wall and was tuned to the local news.

Mrs. Visser was in a wheelchair, her legs covered by a crocheted throw that looked handmade. Her sparse white hair was neatly combed and she was wearing a white blouse buttoned to the neck.

She peered at Monica, her head tilted like an inquisitive bird. Her blue eyes were cloudy.

"Hello, dear. Are you one of the new therapists?"

"No," Monica said, bending down so Mrs. Visser could hear her. "I . . . I'm an acquaintance of your daughter."

"How lovely of you to come and visit." She reached out and grabbed Monica's hand in a surprisingly strong grasp. "Won't you sit down?"

Monica pulled the desk chair out and sat down. She fished in her purse for the photograph and held it out to Mildred.

"What's this, dear?" She glanced at it. "Would you hand me my glasses, please? They're on top of the desk."

Monica handed them to her and she put them on. She looked at the picture.

"Why, that's Marta and Joyce," she said, smiling at Monica. "I can't believe how young they were. I lived next door to Joyce and used to babysit her when she was too little to go with her parents to the Wednesday night church service." She pulled at a loose thread on the afghan. The skin on her hands was thin and blue-veined.

"Marta and Joyce were like the Bobssey Twins, always together. People even called them that."

Mildred looked off into the distance. "As they say, those were the days. Hard to believe it's all over and this"—she waved her arm to indicate the room—"is my final stop. Heaven's waiting room, we call it." She chuckled softly.

"What was Marta like?" Monica said.

"Marta? She was on the quiet side—shy, I guess you'd say. Not like her brother and sister, they were always getting in trouble for talking in class." She giggled. "Marta was a very good student, making the honor roll regularly, and she helped take care of her mother when her mother came down with dementia. Her mother wasn't very old, poor thing.

"None of us ever got into real trouble in those days. Not like today with all the drugs and guns and whatnot. It makes me glad my time is almost up. At least there wasn't any trouble until that one thing happened, that incident, but then Marta and Joyce were older by then."

"What was that? What happened?" Monica said, sensing this could be something important.

"What? What thing, dear?"

Just then there was a knock on the door and a woman walked in. "Time for your physical therapy, Mildred," she said in a singsong voice.

"But we haven't finished our conversation," Monica objected.

The aide wagged her finger at Monica. "We mustn't be late, I'm afraid."

"It's been lovely visiting with you, dear," Mildred said to Monica as the aide began to wheel her from the room.

Monica could have screamed. She had the feeling that Mildred had been about to tell her something that was possibly important. Maybe even very important.

• • •

Monica glanced at her bedside clock. It was still fairly early and there was no reason she couldn't sleep in a little longer, but she decided to get up and surprise Greg with some waffles for breakfast.

She crept out from under the covers, being careful not to wake her husband, and took her clothes into the bathroom to dress. The tile floor was cold under her bare feet and she quickly pulled on some jeans, a sweater and a pair of thick socks.

The water, when it came out of the tap, was cold and Monica let it run for a few minutes until it was warm enough to splash on her face. She peered out the window. It was rimed with frost around the edges of the glass like icing on a cake.

She paused in the hall to bump up the temperature on the thermostat—they always turned it down at night—and then headed down the stairs to the kitchen.

It was still dark out. She flipped on the switch and blinked in the sudden bright light. Mittens, who had been curled up contentedly at the foot of their bed, made an appearance, yawning and stretching in the doorway before wandering over to her dish.

"I get the hint," Monica said, picking up the cat's dish and carrying it to the counter.

She filled it with Mittens's favorite food and put the dish on the floor. Mittens wandered over, sniffed the dish, then, with her tail in the air, wandered off to groom herself in the corner of the room.

Monica mixed the batter for the waffles, adding a handful of dried cranberries to the mix and stirring it up. She started the coffee and put six strips of bacon in the frying pan.

The last drops of coffee were dripping from the machine into the carafe when Greg appeared, his face still creased with sleep and his hair rumpled.

"What are those delicious smells?" he said.

Monica smiled. "Coffee, bacon and cranberry waffles."

"You're too good to me," Greg said, kissing her on the cheek. "I'll get the paper."

Monica heard the front door open and Greg grunt as he bent over to pick up the newspaper. He came back into the kitchen with a quizzical look on his face.

"This was on top of the newspaper," he said. "It's addressed to you." He handed Monica a folded sheet of paper torn from a yellow pad. Her name was written on top. It was the same block lettering that had been on the note she'd been handed yesterday. The sight of it gave her a chill.

She opened it up. The note inside was short and to the point.

Check out that building behind the last cranberry bog to the south. We told you not to sell and we meant it.

Monica gasped. "That's the storage shed where Jeff keeps all his equipment." The paper fluttered in her hand. "If they've done something to his equipment . . ."

"Let's not jump to conclusions," Greg said. "We'd better check it out first."

They grabbed their jackets, hats and gloves and pulled them on as they were rushing out the door.

The air had a knife edge to it that felt especially sharp to Monica after the warmth of the cottage kitchen. The sky was heavy with low-lying angry-looking clouds but there were patches of blue sky that indicated the day might turn fine after all.

Monica huddled inside her parka, hoping that walking briskly would warm her up. But her heart was chilled as well. If someone had done something to harm Jeff, she didn't know what she would do. He couldn't afford to buy new equipment, it would ruin him.

She gave a bitter laugh.

"What's so funny?" Greg said.

"If they've destroyed any of Jeff's equipment, it will be the end of the farm and he'll be forced to sell. Which is the exact opposite of what this person . . . or persons . . . want."

"Hoist upon their own petard, so to speak."

"Exactly." Monica sighed. "It would be funny if it wasn't so serious."

They rounded the bend in the path and the storage shed came into view.

Monica stopped in her tracks and grabbed Greg's arm.

"Look," she said, pointing.

"What the . . ." Greg said.

"I'd better call Jeff," Monica said, pulling her cell phone from her purse.

Chapter 14

Jeff arrived, breathless, his jacket thrown over a sweatshirt and a pair of plaid pajama bottoms. Monica remembered giving them to him for Christmas two years earlier. They'd obviously roused him from bed. Monica felt bad—Jeff needed his rest when he could get it. A farm was a seven-days-a-week job and Jeff rarely took time off.

As Jeff got closer, Monica pointed toward the side of the storage shed. Jeff stopped and turned to look.

He swore vehemently and Monica heard him even from where she was standing. Jeff yanked off his hat and threw it on the ground in a fury.

Monica looked at the side of the storage shed again. The wood was worn and the paint was peeling. Jeff had planned to paint it in the spring. But now he'd have to do it sooner to wipe out the words that had been spray-painted in giant block letters on the side: *Don't sell the farm. Or else.*

It was the same message Monica had received in the note, the one handed to her as she walked down Beach Hollow Road. She hadn't told Jeff about that, not wanting to upset him or to sway his decision despite the fact she was praying he wouldn't sell Sassamanash Farm.

Jeff was near tears. "Who did this? Who would do this to me?"

Monica picked his hat up off the ground and handed it to him, urging him to put it back on. His ears were already bright red from the cold.

"I don't get it," Jeff said as he pulled his hat down over his forehead. "It's no one's business but my own whether or not I sell the farm."

"It seems someone in town has a strong opinion about it," Greg said mildly.

"I didn't tell you, I didn't want to upset you," Monica said. Guilt gnawed at her. Jeff had a right to know about anything that might affect him. "Someone handed me a note yesterday. I was walking down Beach Hollow Road, and it warned you not to sell. Or else."

Jeff spun around and looked at the message sprayed onto the storage shed. "Those are the same words."

"May I suggest we head back to the cottage," Greg said, his hands stuffed into the pockets of his jacket and his collar pulled up around his ears. "I think we'll find it a tad warmer."

They began walking back toward the cottage. Jeff stopped and kicked at a clump of icy snow alongside the path.

"Feel better?" Monica said with a smile. She'd always been able to cheer her younger brother up and she felt as if she was failing him.

Jeff gave a self-conscious grin. "I guess so."

The cottage felt blessedly warm after the frigid temperatures outdoors, almost too warm. Monica felt her face flushing and quickly peeled off her jacket and other outerwear. She immediately got busy pouring out cups of hot coffee while everyone else shed their outdoor gear.

Jeff sank into a chair at the kitchen table and put his head in his hands.

"I feel so guilty. And so . . . selfish for wanting to sell the farm when it is going to affect so many people."

"You have to do what's right for you," Monica said.

She tried to keep her voice neutral, although inside she was screaming at Jeff not to sell. But she knew that was equally selfish. If Jeff had a chance to repair the damage to his arm, who could blame him for taking it?

"And who knows?" Greg said. He was leaning against the counter cradling a mug of coffee in his hands. "Maybe the towns-people will actually enjoy having a shopping mall so close at hand."

Jeff looked up, a stricken expression on his face. "A mall? I thought the developer was going to build a couple of houses here. I'd managed to convince myself that that wasn't too entirely terrible. It would mean more customers for the merchants in town." He groaned and put his face in his hands again. "Now I don't know what to do."

"I don't think anyone would blame you for taking a chance on this new therapy, even if that does mean selling," Monica said. "Maybe if you let people know . . ."

She wanted to reach out and touch Jeff, hug him, but she held back. She knew it would only embarrass him.

"Sure." Jeff swiveled around in his chair to face Monica. "And then if the therapy doesn't work, people will say I sold them out for nothing." He moaned again. "Either way, I'll be a pariah."

• • •

"I don't imagine the townspeople will be very pleased about a mall opening minutes away," Greg said, up to his elbows in soapy water. He turned to face Monica and water dripped down his arms. "I wonder if there will be a big chain bookstore? That won't improve business at Book 'Em, I'm afraid."

Monica chewed her lip. What if Book 'Em went under? What would they do then? She supposed they could move back to Chicago. Greg could go back to work in his old field and surely she'd be able to find some sort of job.

"I suppose it would have an impact." They'd have to do something to make Book 'Em even more attractive, Monica thought. Greg already sold used books, which many of his customers appreciated. He ran several book groups and he scouted out rare first editions for collectors who were willing to pay for that sort of thing. What more could they do?

Monica suddenly had an idea. She was so startled she dropped the pan she was drying.

Greg gave her a funny look. "Everything okay?"

"We should open a café," Monica blurted out.

Greg's peculiar look became even more pronounced. "A café?" he said incredulously.

"Yes."

"Where?"

"In Book 'Em itself." Monica was warming to the idea. "We are already planning to take over the second floor where your apartment is—that would give us plenty of space for a few tables and a counter. I could make the baked goods and we could offer coffee and tea."

Greg closed his eyes as if considering the idea. "But most of the big chain bookstores have cafés in them. Why would people come to ours?"

"The personal touch," Monica said triumphantly. Cranberry Cove residents appreciate going to places where the owners know their names and where they feel welcome. Are they going to get that in some large anonymous chain bookstore?"

"You might be right," Greg said, plunging the last pan into the soapy water. "But let's not get ahead of ourselves. We don't know what Jeff's decision is going to be yet."

Monica paused with her hand on a cupboard door.

"Book 'Em wouldn't be the only store that would feel the competition from mall stores. On the other hand, I don't imagine people will stop going to Bart's Butcher or the hardware store or the Purple Grape — people like convenience and that's what they offer.

"And the mall is unlikely to include a butcher or a hardware store or a wine store," Greg said dryly. "But most of them offer one of the bigger bookstores."

"True," Monica admitted. "But think of Tempest's shop or Gina's. They're quite unique and probably won't be duplicated. But what about the Pepper Pot or the dining room at the Cranberry Cove Inn? A large chain restaurant would certainly give them a run for their money."

"True. Maybe one of the owners of the restaurants is the person trying to send Jeff the message not to sell."

"The Pepper Pot is under new ownership. I'm sure they'd be nervous about the competition."

"Good point." Greg handed Monica the last pot. "I don't suppose we'll ever know."

Monica wasn't so sure about that. A plan was hatching in her mind, but she decided it might be best not to share it with Greg just yet.

• • •

As soon as Greg left to run to the grocery store, Monica picked up her cell phone and dialed Gina.

"Why are you whispering?" Gina said after Monica said hello.

Monica cleared her throat. "I don't know. I don't want Greg to hear our conversation, but he's left for the store. I guess I'm being overly cautious."

"Now you really have me intrigued," Gina purred.

Monica told Gina about the graffiti they'd discovered on the side of the storage shed that morning.

Gina gasped. "Oh, my poor Jeffie. Was he terribly upset? Who would do something like that to him?"

Monica explained her theory about how a restaurant owner, particularly Mickey Welch of the Pepper Pot, might be responsible for the messages meant to harass Jeff into deciding not to sell.

"What are we going to do?" Gina said. "I can't bear thinking how upset Jeff must be."

"That's why I'm calling you," Monica said. "I have a plan."

"I'm all ears," Gina said.

"I think the owner of the Pepper Pot has the most to lose if a bigger, better-known restaurant opens nearby. It's fairly new and so is the owner." Monica paused. She had to put this delicately. "I need someone to feel him out, to get a sense of whether or not he might be the one behind this."

Gina grunted. "I assume you want me to flirt with him a bit and see what I can weasel out of him. What does he look like?" She sighed. "Overweight and bald with false teeth, no doubt."

Monica laughed. "Not at all. He has all his hair and all his teeth. He's not unattractive."

"Short? Tall?" Gina said.

"Tall enough. And muscular."

"Oooh, I like muscular," Gina cooed. "And if he invites me to dinner, at least the food will be good."

"So you'll do it?" Monica said.

"If this will help my Jeffie, of course."

• • •

Wednesday morning, Monica prepared a carton of baked goods to take to the food pantry and carried it out to her car. It gave her such a good feeling to be able to contribute that she didn't even mind the extra work or having to get up an hour earlier to get all the baking done.

Not that it had been easy to coax herself out from under her warm covers into the chill of the morning, but she'd managed it, having hit the snooze button on her alarm only once.

The skies were overcast with dark heavy clouds that portended snow. The water in the harbor was gray and choppy and gave Monica a chill. She turned the heater up a notch and luxuriated in the blast of warm air.

The volunteers at the food pantry had made a special effort to make it a relatively attractive place. The front window was gleaming and the sidewalk was cleared and swept, making it a total contrast to Flynn's Bar next door, which looked even more derelict and dreary in the grim morning light.

Joyce was standing at the counter when Monica opened the door. She was dropping off a carton filled with cans of food and boxes of mixes. She smiled when she saw Monica.

"It's Monica, isn't it?" She turned to the volunteer standing behind the counter. "Monica is my patron saint. She saved me when I was waylaid by the side of the road with a dead battery."

Monica tried to wave the compliment away, but Joyce was having none of it.

"I would have been stranded in the freezing cold," she continued, "if it hadn't been for her kindness in helping a poor old soul like me."

"Really, it was nothing," Monica insisted. She put her carton of baked goods on the counter.

"Mmmmm, those smell good," Joyce said. "Some lucky people are really going to enjoy those goodies. What a lovely treat for them. And how kind of you to donate them."

The door opened and Cheryl DeSantis walked in. Joyce looked at her and sniffed.

"That's poor Marta's cousin," she whispered to Monica.

"Yes, I've met her," Monica said, trying to edge toward the door.

"She took advantage of poor Marta," Joyce said, lowering her voice as Cheryl swept past them and took a seat in the waiting room. "Even on the day she died."

Monica stopped her retreat toward the door and moved closer to Joyce.

"What did she do?"

"I went over to visit with Marta that morning like I always do. I'd baked a fresh coffee cake and I thought she'd enjoy some.

When I got there, Cheryl's car was in the driveway. I was going to leave—I certainly didn't want to visit with that woman there—but I thought I'd leave her the coffee cake in case she wanted some for a midmorning snack."

Joyce took a long, deep breath. "I went up to the front door and knocked. Usually I just walked right in, but seeing as how Cheryl was there I thought better of it. I knocked good and loud but Marta didn't come to the door. It was unlocked so I went inside, calling her name like I usually do.

"Well, what did I hear? The two of them, Marta and Cheryl, going at it hammer and tongs, as my dear mother used to say."

"They were having words?" Monica said.

"They were shouting," Joyce said, putting her fingers in her ears. "It was horrible. And to think that was Marta's last day on earth. It makes me want to cry."

"What did you do?"

"Do?" Joyce smoothed the front of her jacket. "Nothing. The last thing I wanted was to get involved with that harpy." She inclined her head toward the waiting room, where Cheryl was leafing through a magazine. "I put the coffee cake on the table in the foyer and I left."

"And that was the day Marta died," Monica said.

"The very same," Joyce said. "Pity I didn't get to see her. I'll never forgive Cheryl for that."

• • •

Monica thought about her conversation with Joyce as she drove toward town. Had Cheryl been the one who had tried to smother Marta? By all accounts, Cheryl had been angry when Marta asked her to leave, but that had been quite a while ago. Why wait until now to kill her?

Monica drove down Beach Hollow Road toward town. She noticed that there were yellow notices in a number of shop windows. She pulled into an empty space by the diner. She thought she would treat herself to some take-out for lunch. The same piece of yellow paper was tacked in the diner's window. Monica was walking toward it when a woman came up to her and shoved a notice of some sort—yellow like the ones in the shop windows—into her hand.

"Hope to see you there," she said before she continued down the street.

Monica noticed she was handing notices to everyone she passed on the sidewalk. Was it an advertisement for the high school musical? A garage sale? It was too cold for a concert on the green.

Curious, she looked at the piece of paper in her hand. It was announcing an emergency meeting of the city council tomorrow evening at seven o'clock at the town hall to discuss stopping the *potential sale of Sassamanash Farm to a developer*. All were welcome to attend.

Monica balled up the piece of paper and stuffed it in her pocket. So now it wasn't just one person who was against the sale. Whomever it was who had spray-painted the storage shed at the farm and had written that note that was handed to her, this was now a town-wide effort to stop the sale.

Monica was about to open the door to the diner when her cell phone rang. She pulled it from her pocket and glanced at the screen. It was Greg.

"Hello."

"How do you manage to always put a smile into your voice?" Greg said, his tone affectionate.

"Well, I only do that when it's you on the other end," Monica said.

"I should hope so." Greg laughed. "And I can't tell you how much I appreciate it." He paused. "But I didn't call you just to hear your voice, as lovely as it is. I wondered if you'd like to have lunch?"

"I was just about to pick up some take-out from the diner. Shall I get you something and bring it over to the bookstore?"

"Sounds perfect," Greg said. "As long as it's one of their grilled cheese sandwiches and a carton of tomato soup."

"You are such an old-fashioned type of guy," Monica teased.

"Things become a tradition for a reason," Greg said. "See you in a few minutes?"

"As soon as I get our order," Monica said, hanging up.

Gus nodded at her as she entered and she could have sworn she saw his lips move in a silent *hello*. She was convinced the other less-fortunate patrons waiting for their orders looked at her with a spark of jealousy and it gave her a lift.

She stood in the take-out line staring at the spattered and stained menu on the wall. What should she get? She realized that she was starved, which didn't help—she wanted everything. She finally decided on a bowl of chili, which had won the diner a blue ribbon in a contest *Michigan Magazine* had run and which had brought a fresh influx of tourists to Cranberry Cove. And also a side of fries. They smelled so good bubbling away and crisping up in the hot oil in the fryer behind the counter that Monica couldn't resist. She was quite sure she could talk Greg into sharing them with her.

Finally it was Monica's turn. She gave her order to the woman behind the counter and stood aside to wait. It wouldn't take long. Like most diners, the Cranberry Cove Diner prided itself on providing speedy service, something the fast-food chains were always trying to claim they had invented but which diners had perfected decades before they came into existence.

Monica collected her order, thanked the woman behind the counter, gave Gus a brief nod and headed out the door.

"I could smell you coming," Greg said as soon as Monica opened the door to Book 'Em. "You are a lifesaver. I'm starved."

"Ted," he called to the young man he'd hired to help him in the shop. "Can you man the front desk while we have lunch?"

Ted appeared around the end of one of the bookshelves. He tossed his head so that his shock of ginger-colored hair was flung off his forehead momentarily before it flopped back again. According to Greg, he knew the current bestselling authors inside and out and had been invaluable in recommending new books to customers.

They took their bags of take-out into Greg's office at the back of the shop. Greg moved a stack of papers from the chair to the floor and cleared a space on his desk by sweeping his arm across it.

Monica felt her toes curl up. She wouldn't be able to work in such a disorganized space but it didn't seem to bother Greg in the least.

Delicious odors filled the air when Monica opened the bag from the diner. She inhaled deeply and her stomach grumbled loudly.

"You are hungry," Greg teased.

"And that surprises me since I just saw something rather upsetting." Monica pried the lid off her chili container and spooned up a bite. "They are holding an emergency city council meeting tomorrow night to hear arguments against the sale of Sassamanash Farm to that developer, Bob whatever-his-name-was from Shoreline Development."

"Tapper. Bob Tapper, I think he said." Greg unwrapped his grilled cheese sandwich. "Does that mean Jeff has already made up his mind to sell, I wonder?"

Monica shrugged. "I don't know. How else would the town have gotten wind of it?"

"The developer might have met with them to discuss his plans, to make sure there wouldn't be any problems with zoning if he did go through with the purchase."

"Wouldn't the town have told him that Jeff's farm isn't zoned for commercial development?" Monica plucked a French fry from the container on Greg's desk.

"I don't know. Maybe it is zoned for that. Who knows when the zoning laws were passed? They might have assumed Jeff's farm would always be there so it wouldn't ever become an issue."

Suddenly Monica wasn't so hungry after all. She put down her container of chili.

Greg raised his eyebrows. "What's the matter? I thought you were hungry."

"I was. But the thought of Jeff selling the farm is making me feel sick to my stomach."

"We don't know he's going to sell. This might be a preemptive move on the part of the city council in case Jeff decides to sell. The developer isn't going to buy the property if he can't build his mall."

"True." Monica sighed. That made her feel slightly better. She picked up her container of chili again and took a bite.

"I almost forgot to tell you," she said, pointing her plastic spoon at Greg. "I dropped some baked goods off at the food pantry and Cheryl DeSantis was there. She's Marta Kuiper's cousin."

Monica took a sip of her iced tea. "Joyce Murphy was there, too, and she sure had a lot to say about Cheryl."

"Oh?" Greg paused with his sandwich halfway to his mouth.

"I got an earful about Cheryl—about how she took advantage of poor dear Marta." Monica clutched her hands to her chest. "Sometimes I wonder if Marta was really the saint everyone makes her out to be."

"A hidden life?" Greg teased with a twinkle in his eye.

"Maybe not that exactly. But a secret perhaps? Everyone has secrets."

"So what did Joyce have to say about Cheryl?"

"This is the interesting part. Joyce went over to Marta's house the day Marta died. She'd made a coffee cake to take to her. But apparently Cheryl was already there." Monica reached out and took another French fry. She motioned to the container. "Have some.

"Joyce heard Marta and Cheryl arguing. Going at it hammer and tongs, as she put it."

"Did she hear what they were arguing about?" Greg removed the lid on his container of tomato soup, releasing fragrant steam into the air.

"Unfortunately, no. She put the coffee cake on the table in the foyer and left."

"So you're thinking that Cheryl killed Marta in the heat of an argument," Greg said.

"That seems possible, but what about the beta blockers? How would she have managed to get Marta to take them?" Monica said.

"Maybe she didn't. Maybe Marta took them herself. She took too many accidentally and began to get woozy so Cheryl urged her to lie down. And while Marta was weakened and faint from the pills, Cheryl took advantage of it and smothered her." Greg rummaged in the paper bag for a spoon.

"I still think John had the strongest motive though. He obviously needs money and Marta was standing in the way of selling their property." Monica scraped the last bit of her chili out of the container.

"What about Dana? How do we know she's telling the truth? Maybe she doesn't have amnesia at all, maybe she made it all up.

She might have the same motivation as John — money."

Monica dabbed at her lips with her napkin. "Dana has a good job. She doesn't look as if she's desperate for money, at least not desperate enough to kill."

"You never know," Greg said. "Look at her brother. You said he drives a Jaguar and his wife is all decked out in . . . what do you call it? Bling?" He sighed. "I wish I could do that for you." His tone was wistful.

"Don't be ridiculous." Monica slapped him on the knee. "I couldn't care less about bling. It's you I want."

• • •

Monica phoned Kit after leaving Book 'Em and he assured her he was managing fine without her, which she had to admit did give her a slight pang. She had decided to visit Windhaven Terrace again in hopes that she and Mildred Visser could continue their interrupted conversation.

Snow was starting to fall as Monica drove out to Windhaven Terrace — lake-effect snow according to the weatherman on the radio. The day was dark and streetlights were already coming on, illuminating the swirling flakes. Monica flicked on her headlights and turned on her windshield wipers.

A thin coating of snow covered the parking lot of the nursing home by the time Monica got there. She found a parking space as close to the door as possible and dashed toward the building. Nonetheless, she had to brush snow off the shoulders of her coat when she reached the shelter of the lobby.

A different woman sat behind the front desk this time. Monica asked for Mrs. Mildred Visser.

"She's right over there." The receptionist pointed toward the other end of the lobby, where a wheelchair was pulled up to the gas fireplace. She handed Monica a visitor's badge.

Monica pinned it to her coat as she crossed the lobby. An aide was sitting with Mildred and they were chatting.

"Good afternoon," Monica said as she approached.

Mildred looked more frail than she had the day before and her hand shook as she smoothed the afghan over her knees.

Monica bent down toward her. "Do you remember me? I visited you yesterday. My name is Monica Albertson."

Mildred's eyes looked unfocused. She became agitated, plucking at the quilt in her lap. "Who, dear?"

"Monica. Monica Albertson. I showed you a photograph of you and your friends Marta Kuiper and Joyce Murphy." Monica cursed herself for leaving the photo at home.

"If you say so, dear," Mildred said. She smiled.

Monica sighed. "You were going to tell me a story about Marta and Joyce. Something that happened a long time ago."

"Was I, dear? I'm afraid I don't remember."

The aide, who had a kind face etched with deep wrinkles, reached out and patted Mildred's hand. She looked up at Monica.

"It's called sundowners. It often happens to patients with dementia, even those who are only lightly touched by the disease. It occurs in the late afternoon and evening and can cause anxiety and disorientation. That's why I'm sitting with Mildred. She was becoming agitated and aggressive earlier."

"Can something be done about it?" Monica said. What an awful disease, she thought.

The aide looked sad. "I'm afraid not. We try to keep to a routine, which helps minimize it, but there's no way to prevent it altogether."

Monica grabbed an armless chair and pulled it up close to Mildred.

"Do you remember anything about Marta and Joyce?" she asked gently.

Mildred's face brightened and Monica's spirits soared.

"I do remember they were great friends," Mildred said. "They did everything together." She leaned closer to Monica. "Sometimes they even dressed alike." She gave a satisfied smile. "They liked to pretend they were sisters. Joyce was an only child and Marta's sister was barely older than a baby."

"Last time I was here, you started to tell me about something that happened with Marta and Joyce. It sounded as if it was something important." Monica held her breath.

Mildred's expression became troubled, and Monica noticed the aide moving closer.

"I don't know, dear. There are lots of stories, but I don't think they would interest you. There was the one time though . . ."

Monica held her breath, hanging on Mildred's every word.

"Joyce had a boyfriend. He was a bit wild and came from what we used to call the wrong side of the tracks. Joyce accused Marta of flirting with him and they got into an awful row. But then something terrible happened." She rubbed her forehead. "I wish I could remember what it was."

Monica was disappointed. She was certain that wasn't what Mildred had planned to tell her the last time she was here. But it didn't seem as if she would be able to get anything more out of her. Mildred's hands were becoming still in her lap and her lids were heavy and starting to close.

"I think the poor dear is ready for her bed," the aide said, smiling kindly at Monica.

She released the brakes on the wheelchair and began wheeling it toward the elevators.

Monica reluctantly got up and buttoned her coat. She was disappointed. She was certain there was something important that Mildred had buried in the depths of her memory.

Chapter 15

The snow had stopped by the time Monica left Windhaven Terrace. The accumulation in the parking lot was already melting, the heavy dark clouds had moved on and the sliver of a moon was visible in the sky.

She shivered as she cranked up the heat and pulled out of the parking lot and headed toward the highway. Traffic was moving slowly because of the weather and Monica was relieved when she saw the *Welcome to Cranberry Cove* sign. The shops along Beach Hollow Road were already closed for the night. Streetlights shone on their front windows but the interiors were dark and shadowed.

The road was a bit slick going down the hill to the farm, but Monica slowed and made it without incident.

Her mind was whirling with ideas and information. Greg had suggested that Dana might not be as innocent as she seemed, and now Monica was not so sure herself. She decided she would start by verifying that Dana really was employed as a registrar at Michigan State University, as she'd said. Perhaps she was unemployed and needed money as much as her brother did?

The cottage was dark when Monica arrived home. Greg had said he would be late—he'd had a shipment of new books come in and needed to enter them in the inventory and make room for them on the shelves.

Monica spent a few minutes petting Mittens, who appeared glad to see her but who marched off in high dudgeon when Monica tried to scratch her tummy. Clearly Mittens was not in the mood for that tonight.

Monica set her laptop on the kitchen table and powered it up. Her first search was on the Michigan State University website. She clicked on the *About* section, where she looked for Dana Bakker's name to be listed as the current registrar.

Suddenly Monica's computer froze. She groaned in frustration and tried to refresh the page. Nothing. Their Internet was out. Even though the snow had stopped, the wind had picked up and was howling around the house and rattling the windows. It must have affected their connection.

Monica sighed, powered down her laptop and closed it. She felt antsy. She didn't want to wait until the Internet came back up. She glanced at the clock over the sink. Greg probably wouldn't be home for at least an hour yet and she had a container of butternut squash soup in the freezer they could heat up for dinner.

She grabbed her jacket, pulled it on and headed back out the door.

The sky had cleared completely now and was sprinkled with stars. Monica turned up the car heater and headed into town.

There were a few cars in the library parking lot when Monica pulled in. The lights shining through the windows and over the front entrance were bright against the dark night.

A blast of warm air greeted Monica when she pushed open the front door. It felt stuffy inside after the freezing temperatures outside. She quickly unzipped her jacket and took off her gloves and scarf.

Phyllis Bouma was behind the checkout desk sorting through a stack of DVDs. She looked up and smiled at Monica. She didn't go back to what she'd been doing but watched Monica instead, one hand still resting on the stack of DVDs.

She was beginning to make Monica feel uncomfortable. Why was Phyllis staring at her with such intensity? Then it struck her and she nearly stumbled.

Phyllis was still convinced that Monica was pregnant and was looking for any signs that her guess was right. Monica felt her face flush. Soon everyone in town would be wondering and watching, too.

She hurried to one of the desks hidden from view behind one of the stacks and quickly got her computer up and running.

The website for the university loaded quickly and Monica once again clicked on the *About* section. She scrolled down until she found the administration tab. Numerous names were listed but she found the name of the registrar easily enough.

And it wasn't Dana Bakker.

Why had Dana lied about her position? Had she recently resigned or retired?

• • •

Monica was surprised to find that Kit had already started baking when she arrived at the farm kitchen the next morning.

"I couldn't sleep," he said when he noticed Monica's look of surprise.

"So you're still mad at Sean, I take it."

"I'm starting to mellow." Kit grinned. "There's nothing like sleeping on a hard floor to persuade you to change your mind."

"That's good news." Monica hesitated. "Since you're already so far along with the baking, would you mind if I ran some errands for a couple of hours?"

"Be my guest, dear," Kit said, sifting flour into a bowl. "Leave me to it. No need to worry."

"Great. Thanks." She hesitated. "You are a lifesaver, you know."

Kit threw his hands in the air. "Girl, now you're making me blush."

• • •

The drive to East Lansing was fairly quick. Traffic was light at this time of day, the commuters already getting settled at their desks at work. After little more than an hour Monica exited the highway and turned onto Grand River Drive. The Michigan State University campus was on the right. She turned into the main entrance and stopped a young woman wheeling a bicycle down the path to ask for directions.

Monica rehearsed what she was going to say as she drove past the majestic brick buildings toward the Hannah Administration Building, and by the time she arrived was feeling slightly more confident.

The office was busy with a number of students, laden with bulging backpacks, gathered around the front desk. Monica finally made her way to the front of the line.

"I'm here to see the registrar, Dana Bakker," she said, trying to sound confident.

The woman behind the counter looked confused. She perched the glasses that had been hanging from a chain around her neck on her nose, as if they would help illuminate the situation.

"Dana Bakker? I'm afraid she left six months ago. Our new registrar is Jaclyn Morris. Would you like me to make an appointment for you?"

"No, thank you," Monica said. "I . . . I'm an old acquaintance of Miss Bakker's, we were at school together. I was told she worked here and since I was in the area, I thought I would stop in and say hello."

"I'm sorry," the woman said, removing her glasses and letting them drop back onto her chest. "I wish I could help but I can't give out any more information than that."

Monica turned to leave and nearly bumped into two girls standing behind her. They were both giggling, their hands over their mouths.

"You asked about Miss Bakker," the taller one said. She giggled again. She had long dark hair and bangs that nearly brushed her eyelashes. "You didn't hear what happened?"

"No, I didn't."

"Everyone was talking about it," the other girl said. She had her blond hair gathered into a wobbly bun on top of her head.

"Let's go outside," Monica said, casting an eye toward the woman behind the counter. "Can I buy you a cup of coffee?"

"Sure," the girls chorused eagerly. "There's a Starbucks not far from here."

"Starbucks it is then," Monica said. "You lead the way."

The girls chattered to each other as they walked out to Grand River Avenue and the local Starbucks.

The place was busy, and when Monica looked at the menu she was surprised that college kids could afford the prices. She got herself a plain coffee and lattes for the girls.

"So tell me about Dana Bakker," Monica said when they were all settled with their drinks.

"She had to resign her position," the girl with the bangs said.

The blond snorted. She looked at her friend. "More like she was fired."

"True, but the university tried to put a good spin on it."

"Why? Why was she fired? Do you know?"

The girls exchanged a glance.

The dark-haired girl spoke. "She was having an affair with a student, which is frowned upon but not something they could fire her for. I mean, the guy was over twenty-one. But then he posted some . . . um . . . pictures of her on the Internet. When the

130

administration found out, they said it was conduct that went against the university's values."

"And she got the axe," the other girl added, drawing her finger across her neck.

That was certainly an interesting turn of events, Monica thought as she walked back to her car. Dana had been out of work for six months. Perhaps finances were starting to get tight. And selling the family property would have solved all her problems.

• • •

Monica hurried back to the farm, feeling guiltier with every mile for leaving Kit to fend for himself again. No matter how many times he reassured her that he was fine, she still felt she was taking advantage of him.

Kit was humming when Monica walked through the door to the farm kitchen. He had several boxes filled with baked goods and was finishing packing the last one.

"I'll take those to the store," Monica said somewhat breathlessly. "You take some time off. You've been working too hard."

"Well, I don't mind if I do," Kit said. "I think I'll treat myself to a bowl of the diner's chili." He reached for his jacket.

Monica transferred the boxes to the cart and went out the door behind Kit, who was whistling now, his hands in his pockets and his shoulders hunched against the cold. Monica could never understand why he refused to wear a hat or gloves or even a heavier jacket in these frigid temperatures.

Several customers were at the counter when Monica got to the store. She quickly arranged the fresh baked goods in the case and then went to help Nora ring up the sales.

Nora smiled at her gratefully as she filled a bag with half a dozen cranberry walnut chocolate chip cookies.

A car turned into the parking lot. From the sound of it, the muffler was shot and the engine badly needed a tune-up. It backfired once and then the motor was cut.

The shop door opened, sweeping the room with a blast of cold air. Monica looked up from the scones she was wrapping in glassine to see Cheryl standing just inside the door.

She looked to be the very definition of tipsy—her hat slipping down nearly over one eye, her jacket somehow skewed to the right. Even from where she was standing, Monica could tell she was drunk.

She wove her way to the counter, putting out a hand to steady herself and nearly toppling a display of cranberry jam.

Her smile was as sloppy as her clothing and her cheeks were flushed with cold and drink.

"Hello," she said to Monica, leaning heavily on the counter for balance.

She reeked of alcohol and Monica backed up slightly, putting some distance between them.

"I need to talk to you," Cheryl said, her voice coming out louder than she probably intended.

Several customers looked in her direction and Monica saw them exchange a glance with Nora. Nora gave Monica a quizzical look.

"Why don't we go to the farm kitchen, where I can make us a cup of tea or coffee," Monica said, coming out from behind the counter and putting a hand under Cheryl's arm to steady her. She left her leaning against the wall while she slipped on her jacket.

Cheryl let herself be led out of the shop without protest. She slipped on a patch of ice on the path and Monica grabbed her arm, nearly going down with her. Suddenly her face turned a ghastly color and she stopped dead in her tracks. Monica feared she was going to be sick but the feeling must have passed because she began walking again.

They finally made it to the farm kitchen and Monica breathed a sigh of relief. She found a chair for Cheryl, who nearly fell into it, her legs sprawled and her skirt riding up her legs.

Monica got a pot of coffee going and took two mugs from the cupboard.

"How do you take your coffee?" she said.

"Black is fine." Cheryl waved a hand, as if dismissing the whole topic. A sly look came across her face. "You wouldn't have a bit of something to add to it, would you? Just a drop or two to take the chill off."

Monica gave her a stern look, and Cheryl scowled, sinking lower in her chair.

The coffee finished brewing and Monica filled the two mugs and handed one to Cheryl.

"What did you want to talk to me about?" she said as she blew on her hot coffee.

The mug wobbled in Cheryl's hand and Monica was poised to grab it in case she started to drop it.

"That woman came around asking me questions," Cheryl said. "That detective. What's her name?"

"Detective Stevens?"

"Yeah, that's the one. Nosy little so-and-so, isn't she?" Cheryl slurped some coffee. "Asking all these questions."

"That's what detectives do," Monica said, trying to keep the sarcasm out of her voice.

"Well, I didn't like it." Cheryl peered at Monica with one eye closed. "Did you send her around to talk to me?"

"No. Why would I do that?"

"Because I've heard you've been asking plenty of questions yourself." Cheryl momentarily closed both eyes and Monica feared she'd fallen asleep.

Cheryl's eyes flew open again. "You need to tell her I didn't have anything to do with Marta's death."

"Why don't you tell her?"

Cheryl looked at Monica as if Monica had just suggested she sprout wings and fly.

"She ain't going to believe me, is she? They don't believe people like me. But you . . ." She pointed a finger at Monica. "They'll listen to someone like you." Cheryl's head drooped. "They ought to be asking questions of Joyce." She pointed at Monica again.

"Joyce Murphy?"

Cheryl nodded. She gave Monica a sly look. "Marta was giving her money, you know."

"No, I didn't know. But that was Marta's business. Besides, how do you know that?"

"I saw her. I saw Marta giving Joyce a check."

"Maybe she owed her money for something. Maybe Joyce went shopping for her."

"I saw it more than once." Cheryl tapped her head. "I asked Marta about it but she said it was nothing."

Now who was being nosy? Monica thought.

Cheryl frowned and her whole face sagged. "It really upset me when that detective came around. A . . . friend took me out to dinner at this nice place on the highway afterward and I could barely eat my steak I was that upset." She glanced at Monica from under her lashes. "I couldn't tell the detective where I was when it happened. When Marta was killed, I mean."

"Why not?" Monica sipped her coffee. This was getting interesting.

Cheryl held a finger to her lips. "It's a secret. I promised not to tell."

She was swaying back and forth on her chair. The coffee didn't seem to have had any affect at all, Monica thought.

"But I can tell *you*," Cheryl said, winking at Monica. "You won't tell, will you?"

"No," Monica said, putting a hand on her heart.

"Well . . ." Cheryl drew the word out until it was six syllables long. She hesitated for so long Monica thought she had changed her mind, but finally she continued.

"I was at Primrose Cottage. You know, that bed-and-breakfast in town? Everything in there is so old." She shuddered.

Monica thought of all the beautiful antiques Charlie had collected for her B&B. Clearly their charm was lost on Cheryl.

"Why can't you tell Detective Stevens that?"

Cheryl giggled. "I wasn't alone." She wagged a finger at Monica. "I was a very naughty girl." She giggled again. "I was with John Kuiper."

Monica couldn't have been more surprised if Cheryl had said she was with Santa Claus. John's wife, while obviously high-maintenance, was admittedly also young and attractive. But then she remembered what Gina had said about John and his wife possibly divorcing. Maybe he had found solace with Cheryl?

If Cheryl was telling the truth, it meant that both she and John had an alibi.

Chapter 16

Monica wondered if it was true that Marta had been giving Joyce money, and if so, did Dana know?

She decided she would stop and see Dana before going into town to Bart's for some meat for dinner.

Someone had shoveled the walk at the Kuipers' house. Salt grated under Monica's boots as she headed toward the front door. No one answered the bell at first but Dana's car was in the driveway, so Monica assumed she was home.

She was about to turn away when Dana opened the door.

She was wearing gray slacks and the sweater Monica assumed she had bought at Danielle's. She had a pen in her hand and there was a smudge of ink on one of her fingers.

"Monica, please come in," she said, holding the door wider.

The living room and kitchen were much warmer than they had been on previous occasions, Monica noticed.

"I had a man come out to check the furnace," Dana explained. "Apparently it wasn't working properly and that's why it was always so cold in here no matter what temperature the thermostat was set at. I don't know why Marta hadn't had it fixed sooner."

The kitchen table was covered in papers and a checkbook was open in front of one of the chairs.

"Would you like something to drink? A cup of tea or coffee?"

"No, thank you. It looks like you're busy." Monica indicated the table. "And I have to run some errands before the shops close."

Dana sighed. "I'm paying bills. Or trying to. There isn't much in Marta's account, I'm afraid, and she's behind on a number of invoices." She sat down and motioned for Monica to take a seat. "Did you want to see me about something?"

"Your cousin Cheryl came to see me."

Dana drew back. "Cheryl? What on earth for? I hope she wasn't too much of a bother."

"She wanted to tell me something. It seems that she saw Marta giving Joyce money on several occasions."

"You can't believe everything Cheryl says. Besides, maybe Marta owed Joyce money for something. Or perhaps she was loaning it to her? Marta had a soft heart and was an easy touch, I'm afraid."

"Is that her checkbook?" Monica said, pointing to the ledger in front of Dana.

"Yes." Dana began to flip through it. She frowned. "I see Marta wrote a check to cash for five hundred dollars." She looked at Monica. "That's an awful lot of money. Marta's income wasn't very large. John and I helped when we could but . . ." She shrugged. "We felt we owed her since she'd given up any hope of a career caring for our mother. She worked part-time cleaning other people's houses until she was old enough to collect retirement benefits."

Dana continued to flip through the check register. She raised her eyebrows. "Here's another check made out to cash for the same amount. I don't understand. I suppose it's possible she was paying some bills in cash." Dana wrinkled her brow. "But I see checks for the electric bill, the gas bill, even to the grocery store. So what would she have needed that much money in cash for?"

Dana shook her head vigorously. "It's not like Marta had expensive tastes. She bought clothes at the thrift store and ate simple dishes like the *erwtensoep* our mother used to make or *pannenkoeken*, pancakes, which we ate for dinner, or chocolate *hagelslag*, bread with chocolate sprinkles for breakfast." Dana ruffled the pages of the checkbook. "She wasn't one for expensive cuts of meat like filet mignon or beef tenderloin. She would make a meal out of *stamppot*, mashed potatoes mixed with vegetables. I can't begin to imagine what she would have done with so much cash."

"Do you think she might have given it away?"

Dana sighed. "It's possible. It would have been just like Marta to have given money away willy-nilly when she had barely enough to live on herself."

• • •

The butcher shop was empty and Bart was at his worktable behind the counter tying up a beef tenderloin with swift, practiced motions. He looked up and smiled at Monica.

"What brings you in today? I have a nice tenderloin here." He patted the piece of meat.

"That's a bit out of my league price-wise," Monica said. "But I would like a pound of your excellent ground beef."

"Coming right up."

Bart selected a paperboard tray from a shelf and put it on the counter. He placed a piece of wax paper on the scale, eyeballed the ground beef and plopped some on top.

"Right on the nose," he said, transferring the meat to the tray. "Anything else I can get you?"

"That's all, thank you."

Bart's expression turned serious. "What's this I hear about Jeff selling the farm? They're holding a meeting tonight at the town hall to discuss it." He pulled a piece of butcher paper from the roll on the counter and began wrapping up the ground beef. "I would never have expected Jeff to do something like that. The rumor is that the developer who's interested in the property plans to build a mall." He cut off a length of string and began tying up the package. He handed it to Monica. "We don't want a mall here, I'll tell you that right now."

Bart put his hands palms down on the counter. "I have to say I'm disappointed in Jeff. I didn't think he'd sell Cranberry Cove out like that."

Monica felt her face burning with a mixture of embarrassment and indignation. She held up a hand.

"Jeff hasn't made up his mind yet," she said. "He's only thinking about it."

"I hope he comes to the right decision," Bart said, frowning. "If he decides to sell it could ruin Cranberry Cove and all of us with it."

Monica hurried out of the butcher shop feeling chastened. As much as she believed in Jeff's right to sell the farm if that's what he decided to do, she couldn't help but feel for the people of Cranberry Cove.

As she walked down the street toward her car, she felt as if people were looking at her with condemnation, although in reality she supposed it was probably just her imagination.

Primrose Cottage, a white Victorian house with mauve trim,

was on the other side of the inlet from Flynn's and the food pantry in a decidedly more hospitable and upscale atmosphere.

Charlotte Decker, more commonly known as Charlie, had started keeping Primrose Cottage open during the winter even though tourist traffic died to a trickle during those months. But it had become popular to visit the lake during the winter to view the fantastic ice formations that were created when there was a string of days with temperatures below zero.

Monica parked her car with the three others in the parking lot and walked to the front door.

The lobby, which was originally the parlor of the house and which was decorated with authentic period furniture, was empty.

"Hello?" Monica called.

A woman appeared. She was wearing jeans and a sweatshirt and was holding a dustcloth.

"Can I help you?" she said in accented English. Her dark hair had a gray streak in front and was pulled back into a bun. She looked familiar even though Monica knew she had never met her before.

"Is Charlie Decker around?"

The woman smiled. "I will go get her for you." She bowed slightly as she turned around and disappeared through a doorway.

"Yes?" Charlie said as she came through the same doorway moments later. "Oh, Monica, it's you." She smiled. "Not looking for a room, are you? You and Greg have a fight?" She laughed to show she was only teasing.

Monica shook her head.

"I didn't think so." Charlie gestured toward a tufted velvet settee. "Let's sit down. I've been up since dawn cleaning rooms and I'm bushed. There's always so much to do, even with Bianca's help."

"Bianca?"

"Yes. She's Mauricio's sister. She came over six months ago. Their mother died and there was no longer anything keeping her from emigrating."

"I thought she looked familiar. How is Mauricio?"

Mauricio was Charlie's significant other. He had been in Cranberry Cove for quite a while now, long enough to be accepted by the residents, at any rate. During the harvest season he worked on Jeff's crew and the rest of the time he helped out at Primrose Cottage.

"He's well," Charlie said. "He's really happy to have his sister here. She's been cooking him some of his favorite dishes—*caldo verde, bacalhau, bifanas*. He said it makes him feel less homesick."

"So," Charlie said after a pause, "if you didn't come to rent a room, I assume you came for some other reason. Are you investigating again?" She grinned.

"Yes. I guess I am," Monica admitted. "Someone claimed to have stayed here and I wanted to know if she really was a guest."

Charlie blew out a puff of air. "We usually keep those records confidential. No point in getting into trouble with someone's wronged spouse."

"That's sort of the situation here, although the couple is apparently divorcing."

"What's the name?" Charlie called over her shoulder as she headed toward the antique escritoire that served as a reception desk.

"Cheryl DeSantis. But the reservation might have been made in the name of John Kuiper."

Charlie stopped with her hand on the guest ledger. "I remember them. Yes, they did stay here."

"Do you have the dates and check-in times?"

"Let me see." Charlie flipped some pages. "Here it is." She gave the information to Monica.

The dates coincided with the day of Marta's murder. So Cheryl was telling the truth, Monica thought.

Charlie closed the book with a snap. "They were a complete nightmare to deal with. I was concerned when they showed up and had obviously already been drinking—at least she had. It went downhill from there."

"What happened?"

"They got into a loud argument almost as soon as they got to their room and you could hear them all over the place. Fortunately they were our only guests that day." Charlie shook her head. "Bianca went to clean the room but the *Do not disturb* sign was hanging on the door all day. They never came down to the lobby to check out. At first I assumed they'd decided to stay another day but then I began to get worried."

She frowned. "I used my pass key to open the door. I couldn't believe my eyes. The woman was sprawled on the bed and the bedclothes were a mess, half on the floor. They looked as if someone had had a tug-of-war with them. At first I thought she was sleeping, but then I realized she must have passed out. I found two empty bottles of vodka on the counter in the bathroom."

"Was the man in the room?"

"No. There was no sign of him—no clothes in the wardrobe, nothing."

"Did you see him leave?"

"No. I asked Bianca and Mauricio but neither of them saw him either."

Monica thanked Charlie and left.

That had certainly been a worthwhile trip, she thought as she headed home. If Cheryl was passed out drunk the day Marta was killed, then John could have easily slipped out undetected.

And that meant that John did not have an alibi.

• • •

Monica was taking the shepherd's pie she'd made for dinner out of the oven when there was a knock on the door.

"Jeff," Monica said, surprised to see him. "Is everything okay?"

"No, I'm afraid it's not."

"Come in."

Jeff stamped his feet to rid his boots of the snow that was caught in the treads.

"What smells so good?" he said as he walked into the kitchen.

"Shepherd's pie. Would you like some."

He gave a sheepish grin. "I sure would."

"Your timing was perfect," Monica teased as she put the casserole on the table.

"I swear I wasn't angling for a dinner invitation," Jeff said with a cheeky grin.

Greg got another plate from the cupboard and silverware from the drawer and placed them on the table.

"Was it the smell that lured you to our kitchen?" Greg said as he passed the casserole to Jeff.

"Not exactly." Jeff's expression turned somber. "I wanted to see if you were going to the meeting at the town hall tonight. I don't dare go myself—I'm afraid they might pelt me with rotten eggs—but I'd like to know what is being said."

Monica and Greg exchanged a glance.

"We hadn't planned on it," Monica said, "but I'll go if you like." She glanced at the clock. "It doesn't start for an hour and a half."

"I'll go with you," Greg said.

"Thanks. I would really appreciate it," Jeff said. "Although I'm sure I'm not going to like what they have to say."

• • •

The evening was bitterly cold and Monica wondered how many people would be willing to leave their warm homes and their favorite evening television programs to attend this meeting. She was therefore quite surprised to see that the parking lot of the town hall was nearly full. Greg had to drive around twice to find an empty space.

The hallway was filled with people, their chattering voices echoing off the walls. Someone opened a door and the crowd began to flow into the room, yelling greetings to each other as they jostled for seats.

Several people carried homemade signs with slogans like *No Developments in Cranberry Cove* and *Ban the Sale*.

Monica and Greg found a spot in the back. Several people obviously recognized them because they shot her and Greg strange looks, as if they wondered how they had the nerve to show up.

Mayor Laninga tapped his microphone and the crowd slowly hushed. A baby began to cry and a woman in the back muttered an apology as she carried the infant out of the room and into the hall.

"It's nice to see our citizens getting involved at a young age," Laninga said and everyone laughed politely.

The mood quickly changed and soon voices were raised in heated arguments when Laninga indicated that unfortunately there was nothing in the current zoning laws to prevent a developer from turning Sassamanash farm into a mall.

"Then change them," a man in jeans and a flannel shirt yelled from the audience.

The crowd quickly took up the cry. "Change them. Change them," they chanted in unison.

Laninga's face got beet red and he began to look flustered. A deputy in the back of the room moved away from the wall, where he had been casually leaning, suddenly on the alert.

Finally the crowd settled down and the meeting continued. Monica was relieved when it was over. Her arms ached and she realized she'd been clenching her fists the entire time.

"I don't think this bodes well for Jeff," Greg said as he beeped open the Volvo. "Those people sounded as if they were out for blood."

"I have to admit I felt slightly frightened," Monica said, latching her seat belt.

Greg yawned. "I'm glad that's over. What are we going to tell Jeff?"

Monica chewed her lower lip. "I don't know. The truth? I don't want to upset him but he should know what he's up against. I don't think we should sugarcoat it. I'm just afraid it might sway his decision about whether to sell or not."

It was almost ten o'clock by the time they pulled onto the road that led to the farm. The streetlights quickly retreated behind them and the darkness in front of them was inky black and nearly impenetrable.

Monica had left a few lights on in the cottage and they made a welcome glow in the dark night as they went around the bend and the cottage came into view.

Greg pulled up to the cottage and turned off the engine. Monica got out and was walking toward the back door when she felt something brush her face.

She looked up and screamed.

Chapter 17

"What is it?" Greg raced to Monica's side, his face pale in the light above the back door. "Are you okay?"

Monica's teeth were chattering and she could barely talk. She pointed to the branch of the maple tree that hung over her small garden.

"What on earth?" Greg said. He reached up and looked at Monica incredulously. "It's a noose."

By now Monica was shivering uncontrollably. "Yes."

"Let's go inside," Greg said, putting his key in the lock. "We need to call the police."

Monica fell into a chair without even bothering to take her jacket off. She couldn't stop shaking. Anonymous notes were one thing and so was painting graffiti on the wall of the shed, but a noose had a far more sinister meaning altogether. It was an outright, unmistakable threat.

Greg opened a cupboard and got out a bottle of whiskey. He poured a bit into a glass and handed it to Monica.

"Have a sip of this. You've had a shock. This should help."

Monica raised the glass to her mouth and touched her lips to the liquid. She grimaced and put the glass down.

"I can't," she said, putting her head in her hands. She looked up suddenly. "Should we tell Jeff?"

"I suppose we'll have to."

"This is really going to upset him. And he's already upset enough as it is."

Greg had his cell phone out and was dialing 9-1-1. "He'll find out anyway. And he won't thank you for keeping it from him."

Monica huddled in her jacket, her fingers nervously playing with the tab on the zipper, until they saw lights coming down the driveway.

"They're here," Greg said, reaching for his jacket.

Monica already had her hand on the doorknob. She swung the door open and stepped back outside into the frigid air.

A patrol car was parked in back of Greg's Volvo, the rotating light on its roof sending ribbons of color scudding across the swathes of white snow.

A patrolman got out of the car and walked toward them. Monica recognized him from the farm store—he often stopped by in the morning before his shift for a coffee and a muffin. He must have pulled night duty this week. They knew him as Danny. Monica didn't know his last name.

Danny smiled and nodded at Monica. "What seems to be the problem? Some sort of vandalism, they said?"

"It's by the tree." Monica led him to the low-hanging branch and pointed to the noose.

He whistled. "Someone sure was trying to send you a message." He pushed his hat back on his head. The tips of his ears were red from the cold.

Monica explained about Jeff's plan to possibly sell the farm and how the townspeople were up in arms over it.

Danny let out a loud exhale and a puff of steam formed in the air like a conversation bubble in a cartoon.

"Not sure what we can do." He looked around. "There are a couple of footprints in the snow—at least I assume they aren't yours." He looked at Greg, who shook his head.

"I'm wearing boots." Greg lifted up a foot. "Those look like prints from a pair of running shoes."

"We'd have no way of identifying them as it is," Danny said, scratching the back of his neck. He gave an apologetic smile. "The best we can do is send a patrol car by from time to time to check on things. Maybe the perp will come back to try something else and we'll catch 'em in the act." He spread his hands out palms up. "It's probably just a prank. A couple of kids who thought it would be funny given that the feeling in town is running against your brother selling the farm."

Greg frowned. "We didn't find it funny in the least, I'm afraid." He sighed. "But I suppose you're right—there's not much you can do. But we did want to report it and get it on the record."

"Sure." Danny straightened his hat. "Don't hesitate to give us a call if anything else happens," he said as he opened the door to his patrol car and slid into the driver's seat. He gave a brief salute and began to back out of the driveway.

Greg put his arm around Monica. "Come on. Let's get inside and get warm. I'll make us some hot cocoa."

• • •

Monica woke up feeling as tired as if she hadn't slept at all, which is what it had felt like—tossing and turning and startling awake every time she thought she heard a noise. The police might have dismissed the noose hanging from the tree as a prank, but how could they be sure the perpetrator didn't plan to escalate their attacks?

Monica was surprised to see that Kit had a visitor when she arrived at the farm kitchen. He was older than Kit and was wearing worn jeans dusted with sawdust, scuffed work boots and a plaid flannel shirt with frayed cuffs and collar. He had a full beard that looked as if it needed a trim.

Kit smiled when Monica entered. "Monica, I'd like you to meet Sean." He put his arm around Sean's shoulders.

"Very nice to meet you." Sean held out an enormous rough-looking hand. He had a deep, rather pleasant voice.

So this was Sean, Monica thought as she hung up her jacket. He wasn't at all what she'd expected. Certainly he was as unlike Kit with his fastidious fashion sense and ultra-modern haircut as he could possibly be.

"Sean is a carpenter," Kit said with a hint of pride in his voice.

"So have you two made up?" Monica said.

They both looked slightly sheepish. Sean looked down at his feet.

Kit smiled. "Yes. Everything is rosy in paradise again."

If possible, Sean looked even more embarrassed.

"But Sean has something to tell you, don't you, Sean?"

"Yeah. I came by here last night to see Kit, I wanted to . . ."

He mumbled something Monica couldn't quite catch but she thought she heard the word *apologize*.

"A car was coming down the drive in front of me. I couldn't see the make on account of it being so dark and all, but I think it was some kind of sports car. Not something I would recognize anyway." He gave a crooked grin. "I'm a pickup kind of guy myself."

"Tell her what you saw," Kit prompted.

"The car pulled into the driveway of this little cottage. A couple of lights were on but it didn't look like anyone was home. Kit said that's your place." He looked at Monica as if for confirmation.

She nodded.

"I saw a man get out of the car. I couldn't see his face and probably wouldn't have known him if I had. But when he went by the light over the back door I did see he had real silver hair."

Monica immediately thought of John Kuiper.

"He didn't ring the bell or nothing and that made me a little suspicious. I thought he might be trying to break in so I stopped my truck behind some trees and watched him for a couple of minutes. I figured I could call the police if I saw him smash a window or something."

He took a deep breath, as if he wasn't used to talking this much. "I don't know what he was doing, but he had a rope with him. He flung it over a tree branch that was hanging over the driveway. And I know this sounds crazy but . . ." He looked down at his feet. "I could have sworn it was a noose."

Monica felt the color drain from her face.

Kit put a hand on her arm. "Are you okay? Do you want to sit down? Should I make you a cup of tea?"

"That's okay. I'm fine." Monica rubbed her forehead. "Last night when Greg and I got back from the meeting at the town hall, a noose was hanging from that tree branch by our back door."

Kit gasped and put his hand over his mouth. "Oh, darling, you poor thing."

"So that is what I saw," Sean said, sounding satisfied. He kicked at the floor with the toe of his boot. "I knew I should have called the police. I had the feeling the guy was up to no good."

"Why would someone do something like that?" Kit said, his eyes huge. "That's horrible."

"I think it was meant to be a warning," Monica said. "People found out that Jeff is thinking of selling the farm. He's only thinking about it—he hasn't made any decision yet. And people are against it."

"But why would he sell?" Kit looked stricken.

"There's an experimental treatment that might restore the

function to his arm. Insurance won't pay for it but if he sells the farm . . ."

"I guess you couldn't blame him then," Kit said. "Still . . ." He stuck his lower lip out in an exaggerated pout. "I've loved working here."

Monica smiled. "And I've loved working with you. But let's wait to see what Jeff decides, shall we?"

Sean left and she and Kit got down to work. Monica began preparing the Sassamanash Farm cranberry salsa. She'd taken some cranberries from the freezer to thaw and had put out the rest of her ingredients. The salsa was still selling well and had carried the farm through some lean times. Monica was grateful.

Monica was thinking through things as she worked and by the time she'd finished the first batch of salsa, she'd decided she was going to go to Detective Stevens and tell her what Sean had seen. She would also share her own conclusions about who had killed Marta. Stevens might laugh at her amateur attempts at detection, but knowing her, Monica had a feeling she wouldn't.

• • •

Detective Stevens was on her way out but the desk sergeant said she would see Monica anyway, but she warned her not to take too long.

Stevens was in her coat when Monica knocked on her office door.

"Come in," Stevens said.

"I'm sorry. I'm keeping you from something."

Stevens waved a hand. "Don't worry about it. It can wait. I'm interested in hearing what you have to say. You're not the sort to give in to hysterical theories."

Stevens's desk was as burdened with files and papers as it had been the last time Monica was there. The partially eaten doughnut was gone and had been replaced by a paper plate crusted with the remains of a breakfast sandwich.

"I assume you've heard about the incident at my house last night," Monica said.

Stevens shoved her hand through her blond hair, leaving it

standing on end. "I heard about it briefly, but I'm afraid I've been so busy . . ." She waved a hand at her desk.

"A noose was found hanging from a tree branch in my back garden. We found it when we got back from the meeting at the town hall."

Stevens nodded. "Any idea why someone would do something like that?" Her look turned hopeful. "It could have been some sort of prank, although it's not in the least bit funny."

Monica took a deep breath. "Jeff—he's my half brother—is considering selling Sassamanash Farm."

Stevens's eyebrows shot up. "Why?"

Monica explained about the experimental treatment that could possibly restore some function to Jeff's arm.

"I see." Stevens slipped her coat off her shoulders and loosened her scarf.

"A developer made him an offer. The same developer also made an offer on the Kuiper property, but that sale hinged on all three siblings agreeing to sell. Marta Kuiper was the only holdout.

"The developer only wants one of the properties. Marta dying has removed one obstacle for the Kuipers. But there's still the chance the developer will opt for Jeff's farm instead. The noose, along with a threatening note someone handed me as I passed them on the sidewalk and the graffiti on the shed, appear to have been meant to discourage Jeff from selling."

Monica shifted in her chair. "I think the killer—because I think the same person is responsible for all of this—decided to piggyback on the fact that the town is in an uproar over the possibility of Jeff selling." Monica picked a piece of lint off her coat. "The townspeople don't seem to have gotten wind of the fact that the Kuipers might sell their land, which would result in the same thing—a mall they are dead set against being built in Cranberry Cove."

"Do you have a theory as to who this person is?" A small smile played around Stevens's lips.

Monica knew Stevens was simply humoring her, but she didn't care. "John Kuiper," she said succinctly. "He appears to be in need of money so it's no surprise he would be anxious for this sale to go through."

"Hmmm," Stevens said.

"You will look into it, won't you?"

Stevens looked surprised. "We are looking into it, believe me."

"I mean," Monica amended, "you'll look into the incident with the noose?"

Stevens gave an exasperated sigh. "We'll try. We're spread quite thin right now. We haven't publicized it yet, but there's been a string of robberies in those big houses along the lake. The mayor wants us to make that a priority." She smiled. "But I'll see what I can do."

• • •

She'd have to be content with that, Monica told herself as she left the police station and headed into town.

Gina motioned from the door of Making Scents as Monica walked past on her way to her car.

"You look excited," Monica said, sniffing the air inside the shop. "Chamomile?" she said.

"No, actually it's an essential oil called helichrysum," Gina replied. "It's used for speeding healing of wounds. It's antibacterial and very good for your skin. Not many people know about it—they think essential oils are all about lavender, rosemary and peppermint." Gina reached under the counter and took out a small bottle. "Here's a sample for you to try."

"Thanks." Monica dropped the vial into her purse, where she suspected she would immediately forget about it.

"I have big news for you," Gina said.

Monica groaned inwardly. Gina's big news could be something as harmless as the fact that she'd decided to dye her hair or as life-changing as her decision to move to Cranberry Cove had been.

She gave a smile that made Monica think of the cat that ate the canary.

"I had a date last night," Gina announced triumphantly.

"Oh." Monica felt relieved that that was all it was. "Who with?"

Gina twirled a piece of hair around her finger. "Mickey Welch. The proud new owner of the Pepper Pot."

"So you were able to lure him into it!"

Gina leaned closer. "Frankly, it wasn't difficult. He fell hard."

"Did you learn anything useful?"

"Well . . ." Gina paused. "He told me that the Pepper Pot isn't making money . . . yet. He had to buy a new stove for the kitchen and some of the fixtures needed updating even though the place wasn't that old. But he's confident that he'll be turning a profit within six months."

"Did he sound desperate enough to do something drastic?"

Gina shook her head. "Not really, no. He seemed quite confident. Although he was worried about the possibility of that mall being built. Very worried, as a matter of fact. Without it, he knows he'll soon be in the black, but with it . . . he's not so sure."

"Did he know anything about the restaurant being proposed by the developer?"

Gina shrugged. "It sounded like it's one of those places with a really extensive menu, where there's something to please everyone—from a steak to tacos to spaghetti and meatballs." She scowled. "No way a real chef could make that many diverse dishes in one night. I'm sure they're microwaving them." She took a deep breath. "But people like that kind of thing. When you can't decide between Mexican, American and Italian, everyone can have exactly what they want."

Monica felt her spirits sink. The thought of a restaurant like that luring patrons away from the Pepper Pot, the Cranberry Cove Inn and even the Cranberry Cove Diner made her feel sad. Cranberry Cove, which she had come to love, would change, and not for the better.

"And the desserts!" Gina threw her hands in the air. "Of course I never eat them myself." She patted her stomach. "Have to watch my figure. But this particular restaurant specializes in ice cream creations—sundaes, baked Alaska, frozen hot chocolate. That alone is going to draw people. Especially people with children." Gina's expression turned grim.

"Still . . ." She perked up. "I did have a great time. Mickey and I really hit it off. He certainly doesn't look like my type." She wrinkled her nose. "But he made me laugh and the time flew by."

"Where did he take you for dinner?"

Gina looked at Monica with an incredulous expression on her face.

"The Pepper Pot, of course. We had a secluded table that he reserves for important guests and the chef made a special dish just for us."

She smiled at Monica, a coy grin that lifted one corner of her mouth. "And the best part? He said he's going to call me."

Monica was quite surprised that Gina had taken to Mickey Welch the way she had. He wasn't her usual type—her usual type being men who wore custom-made suits, drove fancy cars and had high-paying jobs.

Monica was happy for her though. Who knew if this one date would blossom into a full-fledged romance, but the possibility was there if Gina was able to recognize the fact that money wasn't everything.

Perhaps she had matured since she'd lured Monica's father away from her mother. It had been like one of those old thirties or forties movies, a young girl working behind the perfume counter in an upscale department store seduces successful man there to buy a gift for his wife.

Monica was nearly to her car when a thought occurred to her, and it was so startling that she nearly tripped.

Mickey Welch had silver hair, not as artfully cut as John Kuiper's, but the same color. What if Mickey was the man Sean had seen hanging the noose outside Monica's cottage? And what if it had been Mickey who had painted the message on the processing shed at the farm?

Had Monica been looking at everything all wrong from the very beginning? Perhaps the three incidences—the noose, the graffiti and the threatening note—weren't related to Marta's death at all.

Was she looking for two suspects, not one?

• • •

Kit had outdone himself by the time Monica got back to the farm store. Lined up on the counter were cranberry scones, cranberry walnut chocolate chip cookies, and coffee cakes studded with cranberries and topped with streusel.

Monica felt slightly superfluous looking at the array of products Kit had managed to produce while she was gone. All that remained was to shuttle it all down to the farm store.

Nora looked very pale when Monica arrived with the cart of goodies. She was leaning on the counter with a hand on her forehead.

"Are you okay?" Monica said.

Nora gave the ghost of a smile. "Feeling a bit green around the gills, that's all. It comes with the territory, I'm afraid. Things should improve next month when I'm out of the first trimester."

Monica offered to man the store so Nora could go home, but Nora assured her that she would be fine.

Monica was feeling at loose ends—no one seemed to need her and she was almost beginning to feel sorry for herself—when she had an idea. The rope used in the noose that had been hung from her tree had to have come from somewhere. Of course, it was possible the person had had it in the trunk of their car or in their garage for ages, but it was also just possible that they bought it right before hanging it that night. And it was also possible that they might have purchased the rope in Cranberry Cove.

Monica knew that the hardware store carried rope and so did the marine supply store down by the harbor. With any luck, one of them sold that rope and perhaps they would even remember who bought it.

Once again Monica headed out. Her first stop was the marine supply shop across the inlet from Flynn's and the food pantry, a stone's throw from the Cranberry Cove Yacht Club.

The outside of the shop had dark blue metal siding and a large anchor hung over the front door. The inside of the shop smelled like motor oil combined with the faint brackish scent of the nearby lake.

As usual, the owner was behind the counter ringing up the lone customer's purchases. He was a big man with a ready laugh and a handlebar mustache and was often tapped to play Santa Claus in the annual Cranberry Cove Christmas parade.

"What can I do for you, young lady?" he said when Monica approached the counter.

"I have a question," Monica said a little hesitantly, being careful to choose her words carefully.

"And I have the answers." He guffawed loudly then frowned. "At least I hope so."

"I was wondering if anyone has been in here recently, within the last week and a half or so, buying a length of heavy-duty rope."

Monica wished she could have shown him the rope but the police had taken it away.

He scratched his belly absentmindedly as he thought.

"Rope, you say? People don't seem to have much call for rope in the wintertime. Now if it was summer that would be a different story. Lots of customers come in looking for rope to moor their boats in the harbor." He shook his head. "I don't remember selling any recently. Now last October, that's a different story. I sold some to Mr. Boscombe—he's a summer visitor—but I don't hold that against him." He gave another loud guffaw. "He's a nice enough fellow, doesn't look down on us residents the way some of them do. I can't remember exactly why he wanted the rope, but it was for that boat of his, she's a beauty."

"Thank you," Monica said.

"My pleasure. Is there anything else I can do for you?"

"No, that's all."

"Tell that brother of yours I said hello, would you?"

Monica promised she would and left the shop. That had been a dead end, she thought. She hoped she'd have better luck at the hardware store.

The hardware store had been on Beach Hollow Road in Cranberry Cove even before any of the trendier shops had opened and still had the original wooden floors that creaked with age when you walked across them.

Bill Oliver, who had been clerking at the hardware store for years, was arranging a display of hammers at the front of the shop. He was stick thin with tan, roughened skin and an Adam's apple that stuck out and bobbed up and down when he talked.

"Bill," Monica said, and he spun around.

"Well, hello there. How are things at the farm? Good, I hope."

"Fine," Monica said, wondering if Bill was the only person in Cranberry Cove who hadn't heard about Jeff possibly selling.

"I've got a question for you," Monica said.

"Shoot." Bill put down the pricing gun he was holding and crossed his arms over his chest. "Are you and Greg doing some renovating on that cottage of yours?"

"No, nothing like that," Monica said. "I was wondering if anyone has come in recently, within the last week or two, let's say, to buy some heavy-duty rope."

"I have to say, that's not any of the questions I was expecting." Bill laughed. "I don't suppose you want to share your reason for asking this."

"Not right now, no. I'm sorry."

He let out a breath of air. "Let me see. We did have a gentleman come in recently. I didn't wait on him but I saw him heading toward the counter with a length of rope over his arm." He shrugged. "There might be others, but then I'm off on Mondays so if someone came in then I wouldn't know about it."

Monica felt a stirring of excitement. "The gentleman you saw, can you tell me what he looked like?"

"I'm not real good at describing things," Bill said with an apologetic smile. "And I didn't pay all that much attention to him. I did notice that he had real silver hair though, thick, too." Bill ran a hand over his own thinning brown hair. "And he was dressed like one of them executives—suit and tie, starched shirt, the works. You don't see too many like that around here. Even the fancy summer visitors dig out their shorts and T-shirts when they're here. After all, they come to Cranberry Cove to relax."

Monica didn't realize she'd been holding her breath until just then when it all came out in a rush.

"Thank you," she said, feeling herself break into a smile.

Monica felt a huge sense of relief as she left the hardware store. It couldn't have been Mickey Welch who had bought the rope. It had to have been John Kuiper. Bill had described him to a tee.

Chapter 18

Monica looked at her watch. It was almost time for her book group. Greg ran several groups at Book 'Em and they were quite popular. Monica had joined the one focused on reading classic detective novels from the Golden Age, books by Ngaio Marsh, Margery Allingham and Patricia Wentworth.

She hurried down the sidewalk. The sun was on its way down and the cold wind coming off the lake felt as if it was going straight through her jacket. She reached the front door to Book 'Em and ducked inside gratefully, basking momentarily in the warmth that enveloped her.

Greg was in the process of grabbing the mismatched armchairs scattered around the shop and pulling them into a circle in an open spot near the back of the store.

"Need some help?" Monica said, giving Greg a kiss on the cheek.

"I think I've collected all the chairs," Greg said, running his hands through his thatch of dark hair. "But if you wouldn't mind putting on the coffee?"

"No problem."

Monica measured coffee into the machine, added water and flicked it on. Soon coffee was gurgling into the carafe, filling the air with its heavenly scent. Monica laughed to herself—she'd always thought coffee smelled better brewing than it actually tasted.

She walked back into the main part of the bookstore just as Phyllis Bouma was coming through the front door, yanking off her knit beret and unwinding her scarf. She was carrying a plastic-wrapped plate of cookies.

She gave Monica a rather strange look that made Monica feel quite uncomfortable.

"Has Jeff made a decision yet?" she said, her mouth pinched into a thin line.

Monica squared her shoulders. "Not yet. But I'm sure he'll do the right thing."

As Phyllis took a seat, the VanVelsen twins walked in, their faces rosy from the cold.

"Hello, dear," they chorused when they saw Monica. "Phyllis." They nodded in her direction.

Greg bustled around pouring cups of coffee and distributing them, along with urging everyone to take one of the lemon cookies Phyllis had brought. As Monica watched him, a wave of affection swept over her. She felt it catch in her throat and bring tears to her eyes. She dashed a hand across her eyes hoping no one had noticed.

Everyone was stirring sugar into their cups of coffee and nibbling on the lemon cookies when the door opened again, sending a current of cold air flowing through the store.

"Am I late? I'm so sorry." Andrea Morgan rushed into the room.

She was the wife of the new rector of the Episcopal church in town and was the youngest member of the book group at only thirty-one. The couple had an infant son and she'd told them that the outing to the book group was the highlight of her week. Indeed, she confessed that it was the only outing she was able to manage until Christian was a bit older.

She took a seat quickly and demurely folded her hands in her lap. Hennie VanVelsen offered to get her a cup of coffee and Gerda passed her the platter of cookies but she said no to both.

Monica had a sudden idea. She pulled the photograph of Marta Kuiper, Joyce Murphy and Mildred Visser from her purse. She handed it to Hennie VanVelsen.

"Do you know these girls?" she said. "I know you know Marta Kuiper."

Hennie adjusted her glasses and looked at the photo. She smiled.

"Yes. That's Marta, Joyce and Mildred Visser." She turned to Gerda. "Look who it is."

Gerda looked at the photograph. "We went to elementary school with Marta and Joyce. Mildred was a bit older." She looked at Monica. "We started kindergarten with Marta and Joyce."

"Did you stay in touch?" Monica said.

"We stayed in touch with Marta but not the others, although we still see Joyce from time to time. She likes the Droste pastilles we carry at Gumdrops and occasionally comes in to get some."

"Someone mentioned an incident that occurred that involved Marta and Joyce," Monica said. "Do you know anything about it? It would have been when they were older."

Hennie frowned. "I'm afraid not. We transferred to a Christian high school while they continued on in the public schools."

Monica turned to Phyllis and raised her eyebrows.

"I didn't know them, I'm afraid," she said.

Monica put the photograph back in her purse and Greg began the discussion of *The Chinese Shawl* by Patricia Wentworth.

Talk was lively and interesting but Monica was afraid her mind was elsewhere. Eventually she gave up all pretense of joining in and didn't realize the hour was over until everyone began to stand up.

She jumped to her feet quickly when Hennie tapped her on the shoulder.

"You were daydreaming, dear," she said. "Is everything all right?" Her forehead was creased with concern.

"Yes, fine." Monica smiled reassuringly.

The ladies straggled out one by one and Monica helped Greg put the chairs back in their places.

"That went well," Greg said as he collected the used coffee cups and plates. "Andrea Morgan is new to the group, but I think she's going to be a great addition. She's smart and quite sharp."

"Yes, definitely," Monica said, although she hadn't paid enough attention to really have noticed Andrea's participation.

Greg paused with dirty dishes in both hands. "Did you ever find out anything about that photograph I found?"

"Yes. I met the daughter who had arranged the sale and she put me in touch with her mother, who is in the Windhaven Terrace nursing home in Holland. She recognized herself in the photograph along with Marta Kuiper and Joyce Murphy."

"Was she able to tell you anything useful?"

Monica sighed. "No, not really, beyond identifying the girls in the picture. She mentioned an incident, as she called it, something to do with Marta and Joyce, but before she could explain, she was whisked away for her therapy session. I went back again, but her dementia was worse and she could no longer remember what it was she was going to tell me." Monica brushed some crumbs off the seat of a chair into her hand. "The aide said she had what they called sundowners."

Greg nodded. "Yes, sundowners. They call it that because people with dementia often have increased symptoms in the evenings." He began walking toward the back room, where he had a sink and refrigerator. "My aunt Clementine, my mother's older sister, was afflicted with dementia and we used to visit her early in the day before the sundowners set in. She was terribly young when she was diagnosed."

Monica was surprised that Greg hadn't mentioned his aunt before. She realized there were still things she didn't know about him.

"The good news," Greg said over his shoulder, "is that people with dementia are usually better in the morning and afternoon. So your Mildred Visser might be able to explain what she meant about the incident with the girls in that photograph if you go see her earlier in the day."

• • •

Monica was up by four a.m. She dressed in the dark and tiptoed downstairs to the kitchen. It was bitterly cold—a layer of frost caked the edges of the windows—and she dreaded the thought of going outside. But after a quick bowl of instant oatmeal, she put on her boots, jacket, hat, scarf and gloves and braced herself as she pulled open the back door.

The icy air seemed to make its way through her layers of clothing to her bare skin and she shivered, wrapping her arms around herself and hunching her shoulders against the wind.

She walked as fast as possible—there were still icy spots on the path to be beware of—and headed to the farm kitchen.

She breathed a sigh of relief when she finally pulled open the door and stepped inside. Kit had turned the heat down for the night, and even though the room was chilly, it felt warm in comparison to the outdoors. Monica shed her outer clothing and got down to work.

She tried to work quietly so as not to wake Kit, whom she assumed was still asleep in the storage room.

She was finishing up a batch of cranberry muffins with streusel topping when she felt a cold draft and looked up to see the door opening.

Kit came into the room in his usual good humor, his face ruddy from the cold.

"Oh," Monica said. "I thought you were asleep in the storage room." She gestured over her shoulder. "I was trying to be quiet so I wouldn't wake you."

"Good news," Kit said as he yanked off his boots and exchanged them for a pair of clogs he kept by the door. "Sean and I moved into our new apartment. We were up half the night arranging furniture and hanging pictures. It's smaller than we're used to, but it's quite cozy and I think we're going to like it."

"How wonderful. I'm so happy for you."

"As soon as we're settled, we'd like to have you and Greg over for dinner. Although he doesn't look like it, Sean is a good cook and makes a mean chicken Kiev. And not to blow my own horn" — Kit bowed his head — "but people have been known to say my chocolate volcano cakes are awesome." He raised an eyebrow. "Their word, not mine." He rubbed his chin. "I wonder if we could add cranberries to them and sell them in the shop?"

"It's something to think about."

Monica sprinkled the streusel topping on the last cranberry muffin and put them in the oven.

"I've made a good start on what we need for today." She gestured toward the items lined up on the counter. "So I hope you don't mind if I run an errand. We need some more cranberry banana bread if you wouldn't mind working on that."

Kit gave a brief salute. "Your wish is my command." He smiled as Monica pulled on her jacket. "Stay warm out there."

• • •

Monica had decided she would make another visit to Mildred Visser. Hopefully Greg was right and she would find her more coherent in the morning. She didn't want to go empty-handed so she stopped in at Gumdrops to buy some candy to take.

"Hello, dear," Gerda said in her tremulous voice when Monica arrived at the pastel pink candy shop on Beach Hollow Road. "What can we do for you today?"

"I need to take a gift of some candy to someone. What do you suggest?"

The beaded curtain to the back room rustled and Hennie walked out. She bustled over to Gerda.

"What are you looking for?"

Gerda gave her an exasperated look. "I'm managing just fine, thank you. Monica needs to take some candy to a friend and I'm helping her make a selection." Gerda gave Monica a big smile. "Do you think she would like some *hopje*?"

"*Hopje?*"

"It's a candy made with caramel, cream, butter and coffee." She reached into the case. "Let me give you a sample."

Monica unwrapped the piece of candy Gerda handed her and popped it into her mouth.

"Mmmm," she said around the sticky candy. "I think these might be too hard for her to eat but they are delicious."

Gerda frowned and then her face brightened. "Everyone likes licorice. Some of that, perhaps?"

"I think the King soft mints would be more appropriate, don't you?" Hennie looked at Monica.

"Perhaps some of each?"

"Excellent," Gerda declared with a side glance at her twin sister.

"You know who was in earlier?" Hennie said as she watched Gerda package up the candy. "Joyce Murphy. What an odd coincidence since you were showing me that photograph and asking me about her and Marta just yesterday."

"She likes the Wilhelmina peppermints," Gerda said.

Hennie shot her a look that clearly said that that was a completely irrelevant point.

"Anyway," Hennie said with a sharp exhalation of breath, "poor Joyce is blaming herself for Marta's death."

Monica's eyebrows shot up. "Why would she blame herself?"

Hennie leaned her elbows on the counter. "It seems poor Marta had recently developed a tremor in her hands."

"It's called an essential tremor," Gerda interjected as she

finished tying a ribbon on the package she had put together for Monica. "Our dear uncle Heinrik had it."

"Yes," Hennie said rather tersely. "He did." She sighed again. "The tremor made it difficult for Marta to organize her pills herself. I imagine it would have been nearly impossible for her to get them in those little compartments if she couldn't keep her hands steady."

"It was very kind of Joyce to help her," Gerda said.

"But why would Joyce blame herself for Marta's death? Is she afraid she might have messed up the pills somehow?"

"No." Hennie shook her head. "I guess she wasn't able to get over to Marta's when her pill caddy ran out and needed refilling. She'd already purchased a ticket to a church bus trip to Shipshewana in Indiana."

"That's where the Amish live," Gerda interjected.

Hennie sighed and shrugged her shoulders.

"Apparently Marta filled the pill caddy herself and Joyce is afraid she might have made a mistake and accidentally put in too many of those pills. What are they called?"

"Beta blockers," Gerda said. She looked quite proud of herself. "Marta was on atenolol. It slows your heartbeat, she told us."

"Yes," Hennie said, her lips in a thin line. "I imagine taking too many would leave you feeling very faint."

Monica imagined Marta would have been feeling very faint if she'd taken too many of those pills. And that would have made it a lot easier to smother her.

"Joyce is beside herself, the poor dear," Gerda said. "I can only imagine how she must be feeling."

• • •

Monica was passing Twilight on her way to her car when she had a sudden memory of that man handing her the threatening note. She shivered. The experience had been very unsettling. He had looked familiar at the time but so far she had been unable to place him.

She had taken a few more steps when the answer hit her. The man who had handed her the note was the same fellow Dorothy at the food pantry had said had been pestering Marta.

She remembered his name now. Dorothy had called him Don.

She doubted that Don had had anything to do with the note itself. More likely he had been paid to hand it to Monica.

And if that was the case, maybe he could tell Monica who the person was who had offered him money to be the delivery boy.

Monica thought she knew where to find Don. Dorothy had said he was a regular at Flynn's, and even if he wasn't there now, he'd be bound to show up eventually.

She wasn't thrilled at the prospect of visiting Flynn's again—the floor was always sticky with spilled beer and the walls were imbued with old cigarette smoke—but she was determined to find out whether or not John Kuiper had been the author of that note.

She beeped her car open and got behind the wheel. It didn't take long to get down to the harbor. The water churning under the bridge over the inlet looked dark and forbidding and thick ice had formed along the shore.

Monica found a parking space and walked up the hill to Flynn's. She paused with her hand on the door handle but then finally pulled it open and went inside.

It was dark and it took a moment for her eyes to adjust to the dim light. The bartender, who had a stained towel tucked into the waistband of his trousers, was pouring a beer for a man wearing an ill-fitting business suit. He barely glanced at Monica as she walked in.

She scanned the room, which was virtually empty, and spotted Don sitting at a table near the rear exit sign, which glowed red in the shadowy light. He was leaning back in his chair with his eyes closed, an empty glass on the table in front of him.

Monica walked over to him and cleared her throat. "What are you drinking?" she asked, pointing to the glass.

Don's eyes flew open and he gave a broad smile.

"Looks like the young lady wants to buy me a drink. I don't mind if I do. A whiskey, make it a double." He winked at her.

Monica tried not to visibly cringe. She plunked Don's empty glass on the bar and motioned for the bartender.

Monica thought he might have been surprised to see a woman in the bar but his expression suggested he was past being surprised by anything. He raised his eyebrows.

"A whiskey, please. A double." Monica took a couple of bills out of her wallet and put them down on the bar.

The bartender placed a glass with a good measure of amber liquid in it in front of Monica and palmed the bills she'd put out.

"Change?" he said, raising his eyebrows again.

"Keep it."

Monica carried the drink over to Don and put it in front of him. He'd closed his eyes again but opened them when he heard the clink of the glass on the table.

"Thanks," he said.

His words were slurred and Monica was afraid he was going to fall asleep on her.

She sat down opposite him, careful not to touch the table, which looked as if it could use a good wipe, preferably with a disinfectant.

"You're the person who bumped into me and handed me that note the other day when I was walking down Beach Hollow Road."

Monica had decided not to frame it as a question but rather to put it to him as a statement.

A guarded look came over Don's face. "So what if I did? No law against it, is there? I didn't mean no harm."

"All I want to know is who wrote the note and who asked you to deliver it?"

"I needed the money. You can't blame me for that." Don took a big gulp of his drink. "I don't want no trouble," he grumbled.

Monica made soothing noises. "You're right, there's nothing illegal about delivering a note. I'm not going to tell anyone. I only want to know who sent the note in the first place."

"I don't know his name," Don said, more to his glass than to Monica.

"What did he look like?"

"What does anybody look like," Don said, suddenly becoming philosophical.

Monica stifled a sigh of impatience. "Was he old or young? Tall or short? What color hair did he have? Can you tell me that at least?"

"He was well dressed. Probably middle-aged. Expensive coat, it looked real soft."

So far he hadn't said anything that didn't make it sound as if John Kuiper had hired him to deliver that note.

"Hair?" Monica said again.

"Gray. More like silver."

That sealed it. It was John Kuiper who was threatening her and Jeff.

But had he killed Marta? Monica could easily picture him putting a pillow over his sister's face and smothering her. He didn't appear to have a heart—something quite ironic in a heart surgeon.

Chapter 19

Finally Monica was on her way to Windhaven Terrace. She turned off the highway and headed toward downtown Holland. Within a few minutes she was passing Hope College again and then finally pulling into the driveway of the nursing home.

An ambulance with its bay doors open was idling in front of the entrance to Windhaven Terrace. Monica said a quick prayer that they weren't there for Mildred Visser.

She went through the front door and into the lobby. Two EMTs standing on either side of a gurney were waiting for the elevator.

The receptionist was on the telephone, and while Monica waited for her to finish her call, the elevator arrived with a loud ping and the EMTs wheeled the gurney aboard. Finally the woman hung up the telephone and turned to Monica, handing her a visitor's badge.

Monica pinned it to her sweater and headed toward the elevator. She pushed the button and the doors opened immediately. She hoped that wasn't going to be the end of her streak of good luck.

No one immediately answered Monica's knock, but she heard noise inside and finally Mildred Visser came to the door. She wheeled her wheelchair backward slightly and held the door open for Monica.

"It's lovely to see you again, dear. I'm afraid I've forgotten your name though. Please do forgive me."

"No problem." Monica smiled. "It's Monica Albertson."

"Monica. What a lovely name. I don't think I've ever known anyone with that name before. Please, have a seat." She gestured toward a small armchair covered in a slipcover in a pink print and with a ruffle around the bottom.

Monica had decided to pretend as if she hadn't already asked Mildred Visser about the photograph. It was unlikely she would remember that evening anyway.

"I wanted to talk to you about this old photograph," Monica said, taking it from her purse and handing it to Mildred.

Mildred adjusted her glasses and peered at the photo. A smile spread across her face.

"They were so young then. And so full of hope. That's Marta Kuiper"—she pointed at the picture—"and Joyce Murphy. Neither Marta nor Joyce ever married. They were both flower girls in my wedding. Unfortunately, I lost my Jack more than twenty years ago." She looked up at Monica. "It was his heart. It had never been very strong. It ran in his family. His father died of a heart attack when he was only forty years old."

"So Marta and Joyce were good friends," Monica said.

"Yes." Mildred frowned. She rubbed her forehead. "I seem to remember something happened, something tragic."

Oh, please, Monica thought, *try to remember.*

"It was something to do with Marta and Joyce. If only I could remember. I know it threatened their friendship for quite a while, although they did eventually reconcile."

Monica waited, trying not to feel discouraged. She heard the squeak of wheels as medicine carts were wheeled down the hall and the hum from the elevator.

Finally, Mildred's face brightened.

"I do remember now. I just needed to give myself a moment to think. It happened so long ago, you see, although sometimes I think I remember things from back then better than I do things from yesterday." She laughed. "The other day I misplaced my teeth and couldn't find them anywhere. The aide found them under my pillow. Can you imagine?"

Mildred's hands moved restlessly on the arms of her wheelchair. Her expression darkened. "Joyce had a boyfriend. His name was Matt. Matthew Meyer. He was a good-looking boy with thick blond hair and bright blue eyes." Mildred laughed. "Well, how else would you expect a Dutchman to look!"

Monica smiled.

"Joyce was quite besotted with Matt. I think he was her first real boyfriend. She must have been around seventeen or eighteen, and he was a bit older. Not too much, maybe only a year or two.

"Marta was obviously quite taken with Matt as well. She got all flustered when she was around him. Now granted, Marta didn't have a lot of experience with boys, but this went beyond that. She couldn't take her eyes off of him. He used to tease her about it and that made Joyce mad."

"Do you think Marta was really trying to steal Joyce's boyfriend?"

Mildred tilted her head to the side. "Perhaps not in any calculated sort of way. She was too naïve for that. I don't think she could help herself. She was attracted to him and she didn't know enough to hide it."

"But something happened?"

"Yes."

Mildred turned her head and stared out the window. Monica noticed she had a lovely profile. She must have been quite beautiful at one time in a very patrician sort of way.

"Matt had a boat." Mildred smiled. "It was barely more than a rowboat with a motor but he was quite proud of it. He spent hours working on it and he took it out on the big lake every chance he got. He was a bit wild and liked a thrill so he tended to speed across the lake no matter how high the waves were.

"One day Matt was down by the harbor preparing to take his boat out and Marta showed up. I don't know what her intentions were, whether she had a valid reason to go down there or she had decided to follow Matt. But the result was that Matt invited her to go out on the boat with him."

Monica raised her eyebrows. "Do you think he was interested in Marta?"

"I don't know. I think he was flattered by her admiration. And at times he encouraged it. At the same time, I think he felt a bit sorry for her. Her life wasn't easy. Her parents were so terribly strict and her father clutched the purse strings to the point where they sometimes had to go without basic necessities. So it wasn't all that surprising that Matt offered to take her for a ride. He was like that, terribly kind in spite of that wild streak he had."

"Did Marta go with him?" Monica was engrossed in Mildred's story and had barely noticed the passage of time. The sun had moved from the far corner of the window to the middle and its rays were now shining on the floor of Mildred's room.

"No one really knows what happened but empty beer cans were found in the bottom of the boat and Marta had clearly been drinking when the rescue workers reached her."

"Rescue workers?"

Mildred nodded. "Yes. There was a terrible accident. They crashed into a buoy in the channel. Matt was thrown from the boat and they assume he must have hit his head. He was a good swimmer but still he drowned. That often happens, doesn't it?" She looked at Monica with a sad smile. "It was weeks before they found his body."

"How horrible."

"When the rescue workers took Marta aboard their boat they said that she was quite drunk. No one knows how many of those beers she drank, but it wouldn't have taken very many to get her drunk since I doubt she'd ever touched alcohol before. Her parents didn't approve of drinking and were quite strict about it."

"Did Joyce blame Marta for the accident?"

"Of course. She wanted to know what Marta had been doing on that boat with Matt when she wasn't there. She blamed Marta for distracting Matt when he was driving the boat. Although frankly, it's hard to imagine Marta doing that. And Matt had always been very reckless, everyone knew that."

"What did Marta say?"

Mildred plucked at a loose thread in the woven throw over her knees. "She insisted the outing had been perfectly innocent."

"Did Joyce believe her?"

"I don't think so. At least not at first." Mildred's eyes closed briefly then fluttered open again. "Poor Joyce never did marry. She mourned for Matt and what could never be for so long that everything passed her by."

"But Joyce must have come around because they became friendly again later in life," Monica said.

"I guess Joyce was finally willing to let bygones be bygones."

• • •

But had she really? Monica wondered as she pulled out of the parking lot of Windhaven Terrace. Or had she nursed her anger all these years until it turned into murderous rage?

Monica thought about it as she drove home. She found it hard to picture Joyce in the role of coldblooded killer. It was much easier to imagine John doing the deed. He had a financial incentive to get rid of Marta. What incentive did Joyce have? Surely by now her bitterness over losing her boyfriend must have faded.

She remembered a conversation she'd had with Joyce. Joyce had told her that Marta's cousin Cheryl had been at the house the day Marta had died and Joyce had heard them arguing.

It was easier to imagine Cheryl killing Marta in a rage over having been tossed out of the house. She was living in her car and picking up food at the food pantry. Life with Marta, no matter how stark, had to have been better than that.

And don't forget Dana, a little voice whispered to Monica. She had a financial incentive as well, out of a job and in disgrace. Perhaps she had turned to murder to solve her problems?

Monica groaned. She felt no closer to the solution than she had been the day they'd found Marta's dead body.

She decided to put all thoughts of Marta's murder out of her mind as she drove home. She flicked on the radio and tried to follow an interesting program on NPR, but when she finally pulled into the driveway of her cottage, she realized she'd barely heard a word that had been said.

Greg was at the stove stirring something in a pot when Monica walked in. The kitchen was redolent with good smells and Monica sniffed appreciatively as she hung up her jacket and scarf.

"That smells delicious," she said, peering over Greg's shoulder.

"Arrabbiata sauce for some pasta," Greg said. He kissed Monica on the cheek. "What do you prefer, penne or rigatoni?"

"I'll leave that up to the cook. Is there anything I can do?"

"Set the table maybe?" Greg turned around. "Let me get my things off first, though."

Papers, Greg's laptop, and a calculator were spread out over the kitchen table.

"I've been going over the store accounts," he said as he gathered things together.

"Is everything okay?" Monica paused with her hand on the cupboard door.

"Fine. Just routine bookkeeping."

Monica opened the cupboard, took out bowls, silverware and napkins and carried them to the table.

Mittens wandered into the kitchen, stopped to stretch and then casually walked over to her dish and peered into it.

"I haven't forgotten you," Monica said and reached for the bag of cat food. She filled the dish and added some of Mittens's favorite wet food on top.

"Did you have any luck with your source today?" Greg paused in his stirring.

Monica smiled inwardly at Greg's use of the word *source*.

"Yes. I did learn something new. It turns out that—"

Monica's cell phone rang, interrupting her.

"Hello?"

Monica was surprised to hear Dana's voice on the other end of the line.

"Monica, I'm at Marta's house. You won't believe this but my memory is starting to come back."

Chapter 20

Dana had said she wanted to talk to Monica in person. Monica finished her dinner, put her plate in the dishwasher and grabbed her coat.

Greg looked up from the papers he'd spread out all over the kitchen table again.

"Do you want me to come with you?"

"No, that's fine," Monica said as she searched in her purse for her car keys. "You're busy and there's no need for both of us to go."

Greg smiled at her. "Be careful then."

Monica blew him a kiss. "I will."

The road to Marta's farmhouse was dark with the few streetlights spread far apart. A pickup truck was behind Monica, its headlights lighting up the interior of her car. She wished the driver would pass her. There was a dotted yellow line and a clear view of the road ahead.

The longer the person followed her, the more nervous Monica became. She wished she'd let Greg come with her. Her hands were starting to sweat and she pulled off her gloves. She'd driven this road many times before so that didn't bother her. It was a general sense of unease that the dark night and the persistent tailing of the truck behind her were causing.

She breathed a sigh of relief when she turned into Marta's driveway and the pickup truck zoomed past her on its way to somewhere else.

She was letting her nerves get the better of her. She took a deep breath and parked the car.

There was only one light on in the house, shining out of Marta's bedroom window. That was strange, Monica thought.

She was sitting in her car for a minute collecting her thoughts when an idea struck her. It made perfect sense. All the pieces fit and it tied everything together.

Her excitement mounting, she rang the front doorbell and waited.

Dana was slightly breathless when she answered the door. She was wearing a pair of jeans but looked as elegant as always in a cashmere V-neck sweater and an artfully tied silk scarf. She was holding what looked to Monica like legal papers.

"I'm sorry I took so long," she said, opening the door wider. "I was upstairs in Marta's room."

Dana went into the living room and turned on several of the lights.

"Would you like some tea?"

"No, thanks. I've just finished dinner," Monica said.

Dana put a hand to her mouth. "I hope I didn't interrupt your meal."

Monica shook her head. "Not at all."

"Please sit down," Dana said, taking a seat in one of the armchairs. She tapped the papers she'd been carrying in her hand before tucking them alongside her on the chair. "I found Marta's will. It was in her dresser drawer under her nightgowns."

"You said your memory has started coming back," Monica said.

"Yes. Not all of it, unfortunately, just more bits and pieces. It's like fog clearing and you catch a glimpse of what's ahead, but then it descends again before you can see the whole picture. It's been so frustrating." Dana rubbed her forehead. "I do now remember being hit on the head by someone. It's quite clear. They grabbed something off the nightstand and lunged at me." She shuddered. "I was so frightened. I managed to get away. I remember nearly tripping on my way down the stairs." Dana traced the burn hole in the arm of the chair with her finger.

"But still no memory of who the person was?"

"I'm afraid not. That part is still a blur. When you arrived I was up in Marta's room trying to find whatever it was the person had hit me with. The proverbial blunt instrument." She gave a harsh laugh. "I even looked under the bed, but there's no sign of anything that could have been used as a weapon."

"Perhaps the killer took whatever it was with them?"

"They must have."

"Do you still have Marta's checkbook and bank statements?" Monica said.

"Yes, of course." Dana frowned. "Why?"

"I had an idea about those five-hundred-dollar checks Marta regularly wrote to cash."

"Oh? I still have all her financial stuff on the kitchen table. I'm afraid I still haven't gotten around to filing it all away."

Monica followed Dana into the kitchen. Dana sat at the table and pulled a stack of papers toward her. Sandwiched in between them was Marta's checkbook.

"Did you look to see who endorsed the backs of those checks?"

Dana looked puzzled. "No, why?"

"I have a theory," Monica said. "But I could be wrong."

Dana flipped through the checkbook. "Here's one of them," she said, pointing to the check register. "Let me see if I have the statement." She glanced at the register again. "December fifth is the date so the check should be in the December statement."

She reached into a bin full of folders on the floor beside her chair and ruffled through the contents.

"Here it is." She pulled out an envelope and removed the bank statement and canceled checks. She glanced at the register again. "Number one zero seven eight." She glanced at Monica. "I'm so glad Marta never did her banking online and also that she put her checks in order every month. She was very conscientious like that."

Monica glanced around the kitchen while Dana looked for the check. It was still as grim as it had been when she first saw it. If Marta was able to cash checks for five hundred dollars each, why hadn't she done something to make the house more livable?

"Here it is," Dana said triumphantly, pulling a check from the stack. She turned it over and her jaw dropped.

"What is it?"

Dana looked up, puzzled. "The check was endorsed by Joyce Murphy."

Monica nodded her head. "That's what I thought."

"But why?" Dana stuttered. "Did Marta owe Joyce money?"

"No." Monica shook her head. "I don't think so. Your cousin Cheryl told me that she had seen Marta giving Joyce a check on several occasions. I think it was partly bribery on Joyce's part and partly out of guilt on Marta's."

"What on earth did Marta have to feel guilty about? As far as I can tell she'd been blameless, sacrificing her own life to care for our mother, allowing me and John to live our own lives."

"Did you look at Marta's will?" Monica said.

"No." Dana touched the papers on the table. "I just found it now right before you came."

"You might want to look it over."

Dana reached for her glasses, which were on the table under some papers, and put them on. She began reading. Slowly her expression changed.

"Marta's left her share of the house to Joyce," she said in astonishment. She looked at the paper again as if she wasn't sure she'd read it correctly. "We'd all agreed that we would leave our shares to each other so that the house and farm stayed in the family." She wiped a hand across her brow. "It's not a working farm anymore, but if John has children, who knows?" She shrugged. "They might decide to bring it back." Dana put her head in her hands. "Why would Marta do that?"

"I think Joyce made her do it." Monica pointed to the checkbook. "Just like I think she made Marta write those checks."

"That does sound like some sort of . . . bribery. But why? They've been such good friends since they were children. That's what I've always been told."

"They were," Monica said. "But then something happened."

"You're right about that," a voice said. "Something did happen."

Monica jumped up. They hadn't heard the front door open, nor had they heard Joyce walk in. And they certainly hadn't expected Joyce to be pointing a rifle at them.

"What on earth," Dana said, half rising from her chair. "What are you doing here?"

"I saw lights on in the house. I was worried that someone had broken in." Joyce motioned with the gun. "Sit down." She turned to Monica. "You, too."

Monica sank back into her chair, her eyes glued to Joyce. All she could think about was Greg and how she had to get home safely to him so they could live their lives together.

She felt tears pricking the backs of her eyelids at the thought that that might not be possible now. Not unless she could talk Joyce into putting down the gun and turning herself in.

Joyce must have caught Monica looking at the rifle. She waved it toward Monica.

"Don't worry. I know how to use this. My daddy used to take me hunting with him. I've been shooting one of these since I was a young girl. If we bagged ourselves a deer, it meant we had meat for the whole winter, and for no more than the cost of a hunting license."

"But why did you kill Marta?" Dana said. "You were friends. You said so yourself."

Joyce gave a sly smile. She pointed the rifle at Monica. "She knows. Don't you?"

Monica nodded. "I think I've guessed."

Joyce tapped a finger to her head. "Smart girl. You're right. Marta and I were friends — for a long time. Until that one day when she went on a boat ride with my boyfriend." Joyce's face began to turn red. "I knew Marta liked Matt. A lot of girls did. But he was my boyfriend." She poked a finger at her own chest.

Dana looked annoyed. "But good heavens, you must have forgiven Marta. It was a misunderstanding. You were friends." She waved a hand in the air.

"We were until . . ." Joyce said and stopped.

"Until what?" Dana sounded exasperated. Monica got the impression she wasn't taking Joyce seriously.

Joyce looked at Monica.

"Until Marta confessed what she'd done," Monica said. She looked at Joyce. "Am I right?"

"Yes. Marta ruined my life. I wish she had never told me the truth." She swiped at her eyes with her free hand. "Matt and I were going to get married. He'd proposed the night before he went out on that boat with Marta. But Marta ruined it."

"How? How did Marta do that?" Dana said. "It was an accident. Matt drove the boat into a buoy. He was ejected from the boat and died. It was lucky that Marta didn't die as well because of his recklessness."

Joyce was shaking her head vehemently. "Marta finally told me the truth about that day. She said the guilt was eating at her and she couldn't stand it any longer. She wasn't well, you know. She didn't want to die having lived a lie."

Joyce stifled a sob and raised the rifle a little higher.

"Marta was the one driving that boat that afternoon. They'd

been drinking and Matt suggested she try her hand at steering so she took the helm. She ran them straight into that buoy and didn't have the courage to admit it. She let everyone believe it was Matt's fault when it wasn't. People blamed Matt and called him reckless and wild. His memory was besmirched."

"Joyce, I'm terribly sorry," Dana said, getting up from her seat and reaching for Joyce's hand. "I had no idea."

Joyce backed up quickly and waved the gun at Dana. "Don't come any closer."

"So you were bribing Marta," Monica said. "Did you force her to include you in the will? To leave you her share of the house?"

Joyce's eyes widened and her mouth opened and closed several times before she spoke. "It wasn't a bribe," she insisted. "She stole my life from me, the life I should have had — marriage, a husband, a home, children. She was paying me what she owed me for taking all that away from me." The rifle wavered slightly in her hands. "I did it for Marta. It helped to ease her guilt to think she was making it up to me somehow."

What incredibly twisted logic, Monica thought. Joyce was — to borrow a phrase Gina often used — off her rocker. She glanced at the gun. But that didn't make her any less dangerous.

"I suppose the cash she was regularly giving you wasn't enough?" Dana said, her lip curling in disgust. "You wanted to hasten her death so you could collect on the sale of the house."

"Marta was refusing to sell," Joyce said. "That offer wasn't good forever. If she waited too long that fellow would have withdrawn it and found another property."

He did find another property, Monica thought, *Sassamanash Farm.*

Monica cleared her throat. "Did you give Marta the extra beta blocker pills?"

A sly smile came over Joyce's face. "That was quite clever of me, don't you think? I put several extra pills in her pill caddy, enough to make her feel quite faint. I suggested that she go lie down in bed until the feeling passed. It wasn't hard to smother her with the pillow. She barely struggled."

"Oh, my poor sister," Dana cried, putting her hands over her face.

"I dumped the rest of the pills and dropped the empty

container in one of those food bins that are all up and down Beach Hollow Road. I figured it would eventually end up at the food pantry and might point a finger at Cheryl."

"You set Cheryl up," Monica said. "You said you heard her arguing with Marta the day Marta died. That wasn't true, was it?"

Joyce laughed. "No. But needs must, you know." She looked from Dana to Monica. "And now it's time to do a little housekeeping."

Her smile sent chills down Monica's spine.

"Get your coats, ladies, we're going for a little drive."

Chapter 21

"Where are you taking us?" Dana said as Joyce motioned them out the door.

"Someplace where you won't be found for a couple of days. If then," she added with a cackle.

Dana spun around. "If something happens to me, the house and property won't be sold for months if not years."

"I'm a patient person," Joyce said. "I'm willing to wait. I've waited this long, haven't I?"

She herded them out the door and down the drive. It was inky dark, the moon hidden behind a wisp of cloud. Monica slipped on a patch of black ice and put her hand on Dana's car to steady herself. She had forgotten her gloves in Joyce's rush to get them out of the house and the cold metal of the car's hood sent a chill through her.

Joyce opened the trunk of her car. Monica and Dana looked at each other. Surely Joyce didn't expect . . .

"Get in." Joyce motioned toward the trunk with the rifle.

Dana balked and Joyce jabbed the rifle into her back. Dana let out a sob as she clambered into the trunk.

"You're next," Joyce said to Monica.

Monica put one foot into the well of the trunk. It was awkward and she scraped her leg against the lip as she climbed in. She heard her pants tear and felt blood trickle down her leg.

Dana reached out and grabbed Monica's hand.

Monica dreaded the moment when Joyce would put down the lid. She swallowed hard—she'd never been able to conquer her touch of claustrophobia.

The trunk lid came down with a muffled thud, snuffing out any light from the dark evening. Monica felt her breath catch in her throat but forced herself to breathe deeply to quell her rising panic.

"Are you okay?" she asked Dana as they bumped down the rutted driveway.

"A bit uncomfortable," Dana said dryly. "I know I read something about how you're supposed to get out of the trunk of a car, but for the life of me I can't remember what it was."

"You're supposed to kick out the rear taillights. I suppose we could give it a try, but frankly I think we should conserve our energy. The missing taillights aren't likely to be noticed on these isolated country roads."

"I wonder where she's taking us?"

"Some secluded place, no doubt. Where she won't have to worry about our bodies being immediately discovered." Monica felt in her pocket. "Unfortunately, I think I left my cell phone at home."

"Mine is still on the kitchen table. If I hadn't been so shocked, I would have grabbed it."

The darkness inside the trunk seemed to get darker the farther they traveled. Monica had a cramp in her arm, which was jammed into an awkward position, and the cut on her leg continued to sting and trickle blood.

She was trying to mentally prepare herself for what would happen when they reached their destination. She and Dana would have to be prepared to fight, but how could they after being turned into pretzels by the confines of the trunk?

The car hit a massive bump, jouncing it mightily and causing Monica to accidentally bite her lip. She ran her tongue over the spot and tasted blood.

Now they were bumping over rough terrain and being jostled with every turn of the wheels.

"Oh," Dana cried out after they'd hit a particularly deep rut.

Monica couldn't imagine where they were going. She hadn't heard any other cars the entire time they'd been traveling and now they appeared to have gone off-road.

The car slowed and then came to a complete stop. Monica's heart was thudding as she waited for Joyce to open the trunk. Would she shoot them while they were in the car? Probably not since that would leave too much forensic evidence behind. Even Joyce was probably smart enough to know that.

Suddenly the trunk lid was thrown open and the beam of Joyce's flashlight caught Monica in the eye, momentarily blinding her.

"This is Marta's," Joyce said, brandishing the flashlight. "She kept it by her bedside."

"Is that what you hit me with?" Dana said in a weak voice.

"Yes. It's good and heavy." Joyce hefted the flashlight. "Marta wanted it in case she had to get up during the night or in case someone broke into the house. She felt she'd at least be armed with something."

Joyce still had the rifle in her other hand. She motioned with it. "Come on, get out."

Both Monica and Dana groaned as they climbed out of the trunk and stretched their cramped limbs. Monica explored the hole in her pants and winced when her fingers found the cut on her leg.

It was dark and difficult to see but they appeared to be on a rise that dropped down to a flatter area strewn with rocks. Dark pine trees were behind them, swaying in the wind.

Dana's face was white and her eyes looked unfocused. She was in shock. Monica realized it was going to be up to her to do something.

Joyce marched them closer to the edge of the drop-off. A few spindly trees lined the edge, looking ghostly against the black sky. Monica felt her stomach clench.

"This isn't going to work, you know," Monica said, stalling for time as Joyce pushed them closer to the edge.

Joyce didn't bother to respond.

Monica was beginning to feel frantic. Was Joyce going to shoot them and then roll their bodies over the edge of the rise, where they would tumble to the ground below and be hidden in the scrubby growth?

Dana reached out and grabbed Monica's hand. Her fingers were trembling and cold to the touch.

Monica wondered if she pretended to trip, could she find a rock and quickly grab it? The darkness made it so hard to see. And there was no guarantee that she would be able to hit Joyce, or hit her hard enough to make her drop the gun.

But all they needed were a couple of seconds to escape. Joyce couldn't see any better than they could and wasn't likely to be able to shoot them at anything less than point-blank range.

Suddenly Monica had an idea. It was a long shot, but the only thing she could think of.

Joyce was leading them toward a space between two of the

gangly stunted trees. Monica managed to edge them closer to one of them, forcing her and Dana to have to duck slightly to get under the lowest branch.

As they were going through, Monica grabbed the branch and pulled it with her as far as it would bend. When it would go no further, she let it go. The branch snapped back into place, smacking Joyce in the face and knocking her off balance.

"Quick, run," Monica yelled, grabbing Dana's arm.

They were steps from the edge of the slope. Monica had barely more than a second to assess the steepness of the ground below before Joyce regained her footing.

Saying a prayer, she jumped off the edge, pulling Dana down with her.

They landed hard on the ground and were immediately tumbling down the slope. Monica's shins banged against the sharp edges of rocks and she felt her hands scraping against the rough pebbles that littered the ground.

She slid down and down until she thought it would never end, but finally she hit level ground. Dana rolled to a stop beside her.

"Quick." Monica got to her feet and held out a hand to Dana, who stood up with a groan.

Monica managed to sneak a quick peek behind her, where she could see Joyce silhouetted against the night sky. She was at the edge of the precipice staring at the slope as if trying to decide whether to risk it or not.

Monica didn't wait to find out what she decided. "Run," she yelled to Dana, who appeared to be frozen to the spot.

Dana startled briefly but then followed Monica as they hacked their way through snow-covered weedy growth that reached their knees and soaked their trousers.

Monica stepped in a hole at one point, probably a small animal's burrow, and fell hard, smacking the palm of her right hand against the frozen ground. She stifled a sob as she scrambled to her feet and continued running, her breath rasping and loud to her own ears.

At one point she thought she heard Joyce behind them, but when she risked a quick glance over her shoulder, there was no one there, just the blackness of the night.

"Do you think she's following us?" Dana gasped.

"I don't know. We did get a bit of a head start."

"Do you think we should try to hide somewhere?"

"I don't see any likely spots, do you?" Monica looked around but the few trees were scrawny and not thick enough to hide behind.

"Maybe she'll give up?" Dana said.

"I don't know. We're a danger to her now that we know what she did. The only way for her to escape is to eliminate us." The word stuck in Monica's throat. "I wish we knew where we were and if we're anywhere near a road."

Monica heard a noise behind them and whirled around.

"What is it?" Dana said.

"Nothing. A small animal maybe."

A shot rang out and they both froze. Dana looked at Monica.

"Was that Joyce?"

"I don't think anyone is out hunting at this hour. It has to be Joyce. But it was coming from a ways off. I don't think she knows where we are. Hurry. We have to keep moving and pray we come to a road."

After another fifteen minutes, Monica was exhausted. She ached all over and she would have given anything for a drink of water. She wanted to cry. Would Joyce find them and shoot them in the end? Would she ever see Greg again or Jeff or Gina? A feeling of lethargy came over her and she wanted to lie on the ground and give up. What was the point if Joyce was going to catch them in the end?

Instead, she forced herself to keep going. Suddenly she stopped and grabbed Dana's arm.

"What's that noise?"

"I don't hear anything."

"It sounded like a car," Monica said excitedly. "I think we're nearing a road. We can flag someone down and get help."

The brush began to thin the farther they went until Monica felt gravel underfoot.

"I think we're almost there."

They continued walking and finally Monica saw a thin ribbon of macadam in the distance.

"Come on." She grabbed Dana's arm. "It is a road. Now pray someone comes along before Joyce finds us."

Nearly overcome by fatigue, they stumbled the rest of the way until they reached the edge of the road.

"We did it." Monica couldn't keep the triumph from her voice.

But their victory was short-lived. A shot rang out, the bullet whizzing perilously close before hitting the road and sending a chunk of macadam flying.

"She must be right behind us." Monica stifled a sob.

Another shot, wide of the mark again.

"We should lie down flat," Monica said. "We're making too easy a target like this."

She was about to drop to her knees when she heard the unmistakable sound of a car coming—a car with a muffler badly in need of replacement. The noise got louder until an old clunker came into view, its body rusted and dented and a front right tire that was nearly flat.

Monica ran into the street and waved her arms frantically.

The car slowed and came to a stop. Monica grabbed the handle of the front passenger door and yanked it open.

"Don!" she exclaimed in surprise.

Chapter 22

"May I offer you ladies a lift?" Don said, doffing an imaginary hat.

Dana looked puzzled. "Do you know this man?"

"Sort of," Monica said. "Get in and I'll explain." She all but fell into the front seat. Every inch of her was aching and her palm was throbbing from when she'd fallen flat on her face.

A shot rang out and Don jumped. "What was that?"

"Someone who's trying to kill us. Let's get out of here."

Don stepped on the gas and the ancient car shot forward, its springs squeaking and its muffler belching noise and smoke.

The interior smelled of cigarette smoke, cheap booze and exhaust fumes.

"Is that someone behind us?" Dana said, swiveling around to look out the back windows.

"Do you see anyone in the rearview mirror, Don?" Monica groaned as she tried to turn around in her seat. Every little movement hurt.

"I do see some headlights in back of us. They disappeared when we went around that bend, but now they're back again."

"Do you have a cell phone?" Monica said to Don.

"I've got one of those prepaid jobs. Will that do?"

"Absolutely."

Don pointed at the glove compartment. "It's in there. I don't hardly ever use it. I keep it in case of emergencies."

Monica opened the glove box. She found two empty cigarette packs, an empty pint of whiskey, one glove with a hole in the thumb and finally the cell phone.

She quickly punched in Greg's number and explained the situation. Monica heard his sharp inhalation of breath but somehow he managed to keep his voice calm and steady.

"Where are you?" he asked.

Monica glanced out the window but all she could see were trees.

"I'm not sure. But I think Joyce may be following us. There's a car behind us but I can't be sure if it's hers or not. It was dark when she made us get into the trunk and it was dark when we got out." Monica bit her lip. "I wish I'd taken down the license plate number."

"Do you think you can make it back here?" Greg said.

"I think so. She probably plans to ambush us when we pull into the driveway." The thought gave Monica chills. "Listen. Call the police and ask them to send some patrol cars to Sassamanash Farm. If that is Joyce behind us, she'll get a surprise welcoming committee that she didn't expect."

"Will do. And Monica? I love you. Please be careful."

Monica clicked off the call. She felt tears trembling on her lashes and quickly brushed them away.

"I can't believe Joyce is the one who killed my sister," Dana said as they lurched down the road. "All I ever heard was what good friends they were."

"It seems Joyce had been harboring a seething resentment for years and it finally exploded when she found out that Marta was the one responsible for the accident that killed her boyfriend."

The lights from the car behind them suddenly illuminated the interior of Don's car. Monica jerked around to look out the back window. The car was inches from their bumper—it had to be Joyce.

"She must be crazy," Dana said.

Suddenly the car behind them rammed their bumper.

"What the . . . ?" Don said, tightening his grip on the steering wheel. "I think we need to get out of here." He stomped on the gas pedal and the car shot forward, nearly lurching off its chassis.

Monica closed her eyes and tried to breathe normally as Don flew around corners, hit potholes at top speed and wove back and forth across the yellow line.

She didn't breathe a sigh of relief until she saw the lights of Cranberry Cove winking in the distance. Never had the view looked so good to her.

"Turn here," Monica yelled as they were about to whiz past the road leading to the farm. "There's a driveway on the left. Make another turn there."

Don slowed slightly as he took the turn on two wheels. Soon they were rocketing down the driveway to Monica's cottage, Joyce's car in hot pursuit.

At first Monica didn't see any patrol cars and she felt panic washing over her. All the lights in the cottage were off, including the light over the back door, which she and Greg always left on.

Don stopped the car and Joyce came to a halt right behind him.

Suddenly headlights from three patrol cars hidden in the dark shadows flashed on, as blinding as klieg lights on a movie set. Several officers appeared beside their cars, guns drawn and aimed at Joyce.

Joyce attempted to get back into her car.

"Hold it right there," one of the officers yelled, his finger on the trigger of his gun.

Two other officers hastened over to Joyce and within seconds she was handcuffed and marched to the patrol car that had just pulled into the driveway in back of the other cars.

Monica felt a stab of pity as Joyce was led away. She'd allowed her emotions to twist her and torture her until she had finally resorted to murder. How miserable that must have made life for her.

Greg came out of the house then. He was in his shirtsleeves. He put his arms around Monica and buried his face in her hair. They stood like that for several seconds.

"Let's all go inside," Greg said finally, still not releasing his hold on Monica. "I'm sure everyone could do with a shot of whiskey after that ordeal."

Chapter 23

They were all seated at a table at the Pepper Pot, a sweating bottle of champagne in a silver metal cooler next to Greg's elbow. Monica looked at everyone gathered together and felt a strong sense of contentment. It had been two weeks since Joyce had been arrested, and she had decided that a celebration was in order.

"Here's to a long, happy life," Gina said, raising her glass in a toast.

Mickey Welch wandered over to the table and stood in back of Gina, his hands on her shoulders.

"I hope everyone is enjoying themselves. If there's anything you need, please let me know." He bent and kissed Gina on the cheek before turning and leaving.

"What was that all about?" Jeff said with a twinkle in his eye. "Are you two becoming an item, as they say?"

Gina actually blushed, which surprised Monica.

"We have been going out," she said coyly, taking another sip of her champagne.

"Come on. Out with it," Jeff said.

"Oh, all right." Gina's blush intensified. "We are an item. As a matter of fact, the thought of settling down is looking more and more attractive." She looked at Monica. "Monica, you were right. I'd been chasing all the wrong things—money, fancy cars, luxury vacations—instead of looking at the man himself. And Mickey is quite a man. He's kind, thoughtful, intelligent, he makes me laugh and frankly, he's just perfect."

Jeff leaned over and kissed his mother. "I'm happy for you."

"Let's drink to that," Greg said and raised his champagne flute.

"I have some good news, too," Dana said. "I've taken a new position at the Grand Rapids Community College. I'll be starting next week. I'll also be starting the renovations on our family home, which is where I plan to live. There's a deal pending for the purchase of a good chunk of the property, which will make it much more manageable for me."

"Not a developer, I hope," Greg said, reaching for an olive from the dish in the center of the table.

Dana shook her head. "No. It's a couple who plan to build a house for themselves and a stable for their horses. The wife rides dressage and they both give riding lessons so they'll need room for a fairly large riding ring as well."

"And more good news," Jeff said, reaching for Lauren's hand and squeezing it. "I've decided against selling Sassamanash Farm. I couldn't bring myself to do it."

"But what about your surgery?" Monica said.

"I got a second opinion," Jeff said. "The doctor I saw told me that there are some even newer developments coming down the pike that might prove more successful. He suggested I wait a bit and try for those. He's going to see if he can get me into one of the clinical trials." He smiled. "So there's hope."

"Did I tell you?" Dana said. "John has been charged with vandalism, trespassing and criminal harassment. He's hired some big-gun lawyer out of Detroit."

"He'll probably get off then," Greg said.

"That's quite possible," Dana said. "But I think he's learned his lesson. At least I hope so. He's always gotten whatever he wanted. But this time he's had to accept defeat."

• • •

"That was a lovely evening," Monica said as Greg opened the back door to the cottage.

"It was. And now I'm tired. I think I'll go straight up to bed. How about you?"

"Me, too," Monica said, flipping off the light she'd just turned on in the kitchen.

They went upstairs together, Mittens darting ahead of them to wait for them on the landing.

Greg went into the bedroom and flicked on the light. Monica hesitated in front of the door to the spare room.

Greg came back out of the bedroom and stood next to Monica. He put his arm around her.

"What are you thinking?"

She turned to him and rested her head on his shoulder.

"I'm thinking that maybe this would make a good baby's room after all." She looked up and smiled at Greg.

He tightened his arm around her. "I think you might be right."

"I . . . I hope we aren't going to be disappointed," Monica said.

"We won't know until we try, will we?" Greg said, taking Monica's hand. "Either way, I know we're going to have a wonderful life together."

Recipes

Healthy Cranberry Orange Loaf

1½ cups flour
2 teaspoon baking powder
1 teaspoon baking soda
½ teaspoon salt
¼ cup unsweetened applesauce
½ cup granulated sugar substitute
¼ cup plus 2 tablespoons freshly squeezed orange juice
1 medium zucchini, shredded
1 egg
Zest from one large orange
1 cup fresh cranberries tossed with ¼ cup sugar substitute

Preheat oven to 350 degrees.

Spray 8x4-inch loaf pan with nonstick cooking spray.

Combine flour, baking powder, baking soda and salt. Stir until well incorporated.

In a separate bowl combine unsweetened applesauce, sugar substitute, orange juice, zucchini, egg and orange zest. Stir to combine.

Stir wet ingredients into dry ingredients. Do not overmix.

Gently stir in cranberries.

Bake 35–45 minutes or until toothpick inserted in center comes out clean.

Cranberry Orange Cake with Cinnamon Ribbon

1 box yellow cake mix
1 box vanilla instant pudding and pie mix (4-serving size)
¾ cup water
¼ cup freshly squeezed orange juice
½ cup softened butter
2 tsp. grated orange peel
4 eggs
1½ cups fresh cranberries

Cinnamon Ribbon

½ cup sugar
½ cup chopped nuts (pecans or walnuts)
2 teaspoon cinnamon

Glaze

1 cup confectioner's sugar
2 to 3 tablespoons orange juice
1 teaspoon orange peel

Heat oven to 325 degrees and grease and flour a Bundt pan or tube pan.

Mix the sugar, chopped nuts and cinnamon for the cinnamon ribbon and set aside.

Beat cake mix, pudding mix, water, ¼ cup orange juice, butter, orange peel and eggs on low speed for 30 seconds. Blend on medium speed for two minutes. Fold in cranberries. Pour half the mixture in the pan.

Sprinkle cinnamon ribbon mixture over batter and cover with remaining batter.

Bake 57–65 minutes until toothpick inserted in center comes out clean. Let cake cool on a rack until thoroughly cooled. Remove from pan.

Mix ingredients for glaze and drizzle over cooled cake.

About the Author

Peg grew up in a New Jersey suburb about twenty-five miles outside of New York City. After college, she moved to the City, where she managed an art gallery owned by the son of the artist Henri Matisse.

After her husband died, Peg remarried and her new husband took a job in Grand Rapids, Michigan, where they now live (on exile from New Jersey, as she likes to joke). Somehow Peg managed to segue from the art world to marketing and is now the manager of marketing communications for a company that provides services to seniors.

She is the author of the Cranberry Cove Mysteries, the Lucille Mysteries, the Farmer's Daughter Mysteries, the Gourmet De-Lite Mysteries, and, writing as Meg London, the Sweet Nothings Vintage Lingerie series.

Peg has two daughters, a stepdaughter and stepson, a beautiful granddaughter, and a Westhighland white terrier named Reggie. You can read more at pegcochran.com and meglondon.com.